Ligny's Lake

AN INNER SANCTUM MYSTERY

by S. H. Courtier

SIMON AND SCHUSTER : NEW YORK

M

First U.S. printing

SBN 671-20840-3
Library of Congress Catalog Card Number: 76-139619
Designed by Irving Perkins
Manufactured in the United States of America
By The Book Press Inc., Brattleboro, Vt.

71-09163

FOR

Pam, Rosemary and Graham

OUTLINE OF LIGNY'S LAKE

1

The quest for Lewis Ligny began the night I saw him in Melbourne, five hundred miles from the place where the same day he was alleged to have drowned. My involvement with him, however, had its genesis long before in my custom of sandwiching holidays between jobs with my married sister in Canberra. Stella and her husband, Dan Hilary, who has some status in the Attorney General's Department, have their home on Mugga Way, and Ligny was their next-door neighbor, and so I had to meet him sooner or later.

Like Dan, he was a civil servant, in his case an engineer working for the Department of Supply on the Deep Space Tracking projects. Over the course of three years, I had learned to like him and I gathered he liked me in return. Perhaps he felt a kind of bond between us. I am also an engineer, or, more exactly, a free-lance entrepreneur for engineering ventures in the minor league of shire road making and dam sinking. I merely hire men and machines, set them to work and when the job is done, dispose of both until the next contract comes up; and for me home is the caravan I cart around from job to job. I suspect this comparative freedom appealed to Ligny, but I prefer to think the true reason for his liking me was I had shown no sign of reaction when I saw him for the first time.

Stella and Dan had briefed me, for all too many people could only stare at him as if he were a freak. He was a big man, but you forgot his size in the havoc of his face. You saw the great warped nose, the red bristling brows half-seared away, the gapped jaw, the seamed cheeks glistening with scar tissue, the graying bronze hair cultivated in a Byronic wave to hide a cicatrix on the forehead, the hard blue eyes that (to my mind, anyway) always held a silent appeal—you saw it all and you felt dismay or curiosity or compassion according to the way you were built. I felt both dismay and compassion, but I didn't stare.

I understood from Dan Hilary this desolation was an aftermath of World War II. Serving in an apparently esoteric branch of the army, Ligny had come out of some desperate enterprise with the George Cross and his face permanently disfigured. He never talked about the war, and Dan warned me that if I wished to make him an enemy for life, all I had to do was ask him how he came to be decorated for bravery.

He lived alone in his big home. A staid widow, Mrs. Jeffries, appeared four or five days a week to do the household chores, but except for breakfast, he ate in restaurants. I surmised this eating out was a kind of inuring of himself to people staring at him, but whether my notion was right or wrong, his home was surprisingly cheerful, for he was an expert gardener, and so his rooms were full of seasonal blooms he had grown himself.

His establishment, however, was more remarkable for an astonishing toy. In a large annex at the rear, Ligny had created a miniature engineering complex, the central feature of which was a pond or lake that strangely resembled in outline a Merino ewe with only one leg—a foreleg. About fifteen feet across and thirty feet long, the lake was furnished with cliffs, bays, capes, promontories, little ports and model ships tied up to wharves. Behind the ports were mines excavated in hills from which conveyor belts dropped down to the wharves, and around the lake was a complicated system of railways that, in linking the ports, passed over bridges and dived into tunnels.

This Lilliputian world was controlled from a console of electric switches placed so that the operator could see everything that went on. Though Ligny always masked his feelings, he did not hide his intense delight when his touch on the switches sent trains racing along the tracks, the conveyor belts cascading minute grains of ore into holds, and ships voyaging over the lake. I'll never forget my own exhilaration whenever Ligny let me have a go myself at the console.

But there was more to Ligny than a clever aptitude for mechanical invention. His study was quite as interesting. Wide, high, brilliantly lighted, it had space for two desks, a long worktable, a big wooden cabinet with shallow drawers filled with plans and specifications, stands of scientific and engineering journals and racks of the instruments you would expect to find in an engineer's den.

Besides, there were his books—fiction, technical works, poetry, essays—piled high on long shelves. On my third or fourth visit to Ligny's place, I lighted on an intriguing discovery, a small red-bound copy of Thoreau's *Walden,* which had seemingly been an English prize given to a schoolgirl called Rhoda Hancock in the faraway year of 1900.

I also possessed a copy of *Walden,* but unlike mine, Ligny's contained two illustrations, one a portrait of Thoreau on the frontispiece, guarded by tissue paper; the second the plan Thoreau drew of Walden Pond in 1846. Some very young member of Rhoda's family, Wesley Griffon Hancock, had printed his name across the portrait, but it was the plan that intrigued me because it bore a striking resemblance to the outline of Ligny's lake in the annex: both had the same silhouette of a one-legged Merino ewe.

I did not inquire into the likeness or into the identities of

Rhoda Hancock and Wesley Griffon Hancock. Ligny wasn't a man to tolerate inquisitiveness. Besides, I had no wish to find out what made him tick—not at that stage of the game. If he volunteered information about himself, well and good; if not, he was entitled to his personal business without intrusion from me or anybody else. Thus, when I would return to Victoria from my trips to Canberra, I usually put Ligny out of my mind, and when I did think of him, it was merely as a queer though likeable bird.

Then my detached attitude toward Ligny fled forever. Having just completed a contract in the country, I parked my caravan in my usual custom with Len and Beth Marchmont at Seymour—the Marchmonts run a caravan park there—and drove on to Melbourne. I booked into a motel, had dinner and taxied to the fights at Festival Hall. The star attraction of the night was Red Aherne, the heavyweight champion, defending his title for the umpteenth time. I didn't care a hoot about Red Aherne. I wanted only to view the performance of a lad I knew in one of the preliminaries, but because of the champion, the stadium was packed by yelling fans, and so it was a fluke that I spotted Ligny halfway through the main supporting bout.

He was sitting in the second row behind the red corner, and I was on the end of the fifth tier counterclockwise from him. Nevertheless I knew him; there was no mistaking the big body, the graying Byronic hair, the marred face—especially the marred face.

Overcoming the surprise of seeing him so far from home, I took out my pocketbook and scribbled a note to the effect we would get together at the next intermission. To make doubly sure he would know whom the missive came from, I printed my name, Sandy Carmichael, in capitals. I gave the note (with a dollar tip) to a passing strong arm attendant, and he undertook the delivery of the message.

To my amazement, Ligny appeared not to recognize me. He stood up, looked in the direction of the bouncer's finger indicating me, scowled, resumed his seat and wrote something on the scrap of paper I had sent him. Twenty seconds later, I was studying the reply—two terse words:

"Wrong man."

When I looked again at the second row behind the red corner, Ligny was gone.

I sat simmering through the rest of the program. There was no disgrace for either man or woman being seen in the company of Sandy Carmichael, and I didn't like being snubbed. My pique rode with me back to my motel in Parkville and it persisted until I tuned into the late TV news to hear that Ligny was missing, presumed drowned.

According to the announcer, Mr. Lewis Ligny had set out from Canberra early this morning to spend the day rockfishing near Batemans Bay. His car had been found and his fishing gear recovered, but there was no sign of Ligny himself. It was feared a wave had washed him from the rocks. Mr. Ligny, a senior officer in the Department of Supply, was fifty-three. He was unmarried. A captain in the Second World War, he had won the George Cross for extreme heroism. Batemans Bay police were continuing the search.

I was galvanized, astonished and nonplused in turn, and then I was suddenly afraid. If Ligny had been washed today from the rocks at Batemans Bay, then I had seen a ghost in Festival Hall. But I had seen no ghost (I still had in my pocket the paper that carried my message and its reply, "Wrong man"), so what on earth had happened at Batemans Bay?

There came a more urgent thought. Of all the thousands of people who must have listened to the news, I was probably the sole person, apart from Ligny himself, to know the announcement was false.

For a while, I engaged in furious debate with myself over what I should do. Common sense urged me to do nothing. Common sense told me I had *not* seen Ligny at Festival Hall, that I had merely encountered a chance similarity of two men

13

of extraordinary appearance, that I should now forget the whole business and go about my own business and not buy into a row that could be nasty and sticky.

Against this, I kept thinking of the appeal of Ligny's blue eyes gazing out of his disfigured face. An appeal—for revenge or reparation or sympathy or restitution or forgiveness, I couldn't determine; but I told common sense it was a liar, that I had really seen Ligny at Festival Hall—that, whatever I did or did not do, I could never forget and I would have to endure lifelong were I to wash my hands of him. To hell with common sense, and I lifted my room telephone and asked the girl in the motel office to call Dan Hilary's number in Canberra.

Dan's voice came on to the line with gratifying promptness. Dan, who had already heard the news from Batemans Bay, listened to my story without interruption. At the end, he asked me to hang up, saying he would ring me back in ten minutes or so. I had to wait twenty-five. I guessed that in the interim he had consulted top brass, for he now wanted me to fly to Canberra in the morning "at government expense"; a certain Mr. Edmund Martin wished to talk with me, and I mustn't forget to bring along the note I had exchanged with my friend (Dan's phrase) in Festival Hall.

That was Friday, August 15. The next day, I stole Lewis Ligny's copy of Thoreau's *Walden or Life in the Woods*. I committed the theft in Ligny's den while Dan and Mr. Edmund Martin were fossicking among Ligny's papers and Stella and Ligny's staid housekeeper were brewing morning tea in the kitchen and a pair of Commonwealth policemen were keeping vigil in Ligny's garden.

I was sorry for the policemen out in the garden. Cold clouds tumbled over Canberra, and a bitter wind howled down from the Snowy Mountains to torment the city and bait Lake Burley Griffin into fury. It whined over Ligny's roof and harried Ligny's garden, but whether in lament or in

14

execration I couldn't determine and nobody would tell me.

Nobody told me anything, not even the important Edmund Martin. He proved to be a blond, tousled, thickset man, altogether different from Dan, who was tall and elegant. I met him after Dan had driven me to Ligny's place from the airport, and I decided I didn't like him, though he thanked me profusely for traveling so speedily all the way from Melbourne and for the paper that held my Festival Hall message and its brief reply.

But both Martin and Dan, although so dissimilar in looks, were one and indissolvable in an affably rigorous refusal to discuss Ligny. In the plane from Melbourne I had been dead sure I would be grilled about the Festival Hall incident. I had been just as confident I would get the answers (or some of them) to the questions that had plagued me ever since the announcement of Ligny's disappearance, and I had jotted down the important ones.

Did officialdom believe I had really seen Ligny at Festival Hall or did it believe Ligny was in the sea at Batemans Bay?

If the former, did officialdom think Ligny had skipped out because of some malpractice?

When did Stella and/or Dan (the missing man's neighbors) see Ligny last? (To be at Festival Hall last night after arranging for his car and fishing gear to be found at Batemans Bay five hundred miles from Melbourne, Ligny must have started out from home the previous night at the latest.)

Had an unknown person been drowned or disposed of in some other way at Batemans Bay?

Did Ligny have any relatives?

Had he made a will?

What was going to happen to the house, the books and that magnificent engineering toy in the annex?

I could have compiled another raft of queries in Ligny's study (some, for instance, about the reasons for the policemen in the garden), but defeated by Martin and Dan's cheerfully impenetrable demeanor, my thirst for information wasn't worth a damn. Stella professed to know nothing, and I hadn't the nerve to question Mrs. Jeffries.

As for the expected grilling, it boiled down to one simple, innocuous inquiry made by Martin as I handed over the note that was my sole tangible memento of Festival Hall.

"Are you a devotee of the fighting game?" he asked, and he smiled as he slipped the note into his wallet.

"Not particularly," I replied. "I went to Festival Hall merely because I knew one of the preliminary fighters."

"Ah?" Martin still smiled.

"The lad used to work for me in one of my road-making gangs, and he was always at me to watch him in the ring."

"What happened to him last night?"

"He was knocked out," I said.

Martin laughed and so did my brother-in-law, and that was the sum total of my grilling. As I watched them searching through Ligny's papers (how that marred face would have reacted to this!) and listened to their urbane jesting conversation, I recalled that Stella had once told me Dan was a very easy man to live with, but she had discovered he was particularly amiable when sudden crises arose in his department. His cheerfulness was his shield against the slings and arrows of misfortune, Stella had averred.

All right, an official crisis was now on both Dan and the tangle-haired Martin, and the crisis was Ligny, but they weren't going to admit me into the secret. Therefore, rightly or wrongly, I pinched Thoreau's *Walden* because of the plan it contained of Walden Pond. While Martin and Dan were laughing over one of their quips, I whipped the book from its shelf and shoved it into my inside coat pocket, where it managed to fit snugly. Moving away from the shelf it had stood on, I broke into my companions' banter.

"This is possibly my last chance to look inside Mr. Ligny's place," I said. "So any objection to my playing around with the trains and ships in the annex?"

Martin looked up from the drawer he was rummaging in like a terrier disinterring a bone.

"Not the slightest," he said. "What about you, Dan?"

My brother-in-law also had no objection. "Do what you like, laddie," he said kindly.

I thought, You bloody hypocrites! I walked out into the passage and hesitated, contemplating stealing back to the door to catch them poring over the note I had brought and comparing the writing of the words "Wrong man" with the writing in Ligny's papers. That surely was the only reason they had sent for me.

But I knew that wouldn't have done, and I proceeded past bedrooms and sitting room and dining room. At the kitchen my sister appeared in the doorway and inquired where I was going.

"To play with trains," I said. "Any trouble?"

"No trouble," Stella said, smoothing her chestnut hair. "But we'll be pouring tea in a few minutes."

"I'll be in the annex," I said.

I emerged onto the back veranda and went to the annex twenty yards away. On warm, sunny days, this was a pleasant quarter of Ligny's establishment. In one direction you could look up at Red Hill, blocking out the dark blue ranges to the south; the other way you could look down over the lake and the city; or you could sit and admire Ligny's flowers right at hand but with the wintry wind whooping down from Mount Koscuisko, this was no place for dawdling.

Besides, I was impatient to pull Thoreau's book from my pocket and, face to face as it were, compare the plan of Walden Pond with Ligny's lake. With Ligny, there was little possibility of things happening by chance—not in any event under his control. Therefore there had been motive and purpose in constructing his model lake in the image of Walden Pond. I felt he had symbolized here an occurrence or experience of momentous importance to himself. In effect, he had fashioned in the lake a kind of icon.

I hurried into the annex, shut the door against the wind and switched on the ceiling lamps. I placed myself at the console, took a glance over lake and ports and railway lines and reached for the book in my inside pocket. Then I swore under my breath. There were two windows in the annex, one at each end of the room. The window on the right was small. The other was wide, and it afforded a view of Ligny's creeper-covered fernery. Out of the corner of my eye, I caught sight of one of the policemen, ensconced among the ferns. I guessed he had hidden himself there away from the wind, but now he was staring in at me.

There could be no flourishing of Thoreau before the cop's curious gaze. I bent over the console, selected appropriate switches and sent two trains coursing around the lake in opposite directions. And at once, despite my purpose, I was again enthralled by Ligny's beautiful conception—the craftsmanship, the symmetry, above all the sense of power in being able to put this little world into operation. Ligny had known this too but in a far greater degree: he had been the creator and designer.

The trains raced around the lake. Ignoring the policeman, whose face was now against the window, I forced myself back to contemplation of the lake itself. I studied the lake's sheep-like outline and the cliffs and capes and bays. There were three model ports approximately equidistant around the lake. I fixed their positions in my mind and the contours of the hills and valley as well, so that afterwards, when I had the chance to study Thoreau's plan on my own, I could combine lake and plan into one picture.

I had already thought of Ligny's lake as a symbol. Now I comprehended that both lake and plan had served to remind Ligny of an actual scene he knew well—too well, perhaps. The thought occurred that this scene was not far away from Canberra, but the notion didn't stand up to inspection. Stella and Dan had seen Ligny's lake many a time, and they were also well acquainted with Canberra and environs. In the days before the subject of Ligny became taboo, they would have spoken of it if the model bore a resemblance to any local feature. In those days they *had* talked about Ligny.

Therefore the actual scene that was the basis of Ligny's lake had to be so remote the connection could never be picked up in the general run of things. Such an idea couldn't have dawned on me but for my chancing on Ligny's copy of *Walden*. So the prototype of Ligny's lake could be anywhere in the world, and the only person who could say where it lay was Ligny himself.

A dead-end street, Carmichael.

I straightened up to discover there were *two* faces peering in at me. The first policeman had called his mate to share in the fun, and now they were both staring at me as though I had suffered a cataleptic fit. All right, I thought; no more trancelike concentration in front of witnesses. I waved to the policemen with false geniality and twiddled the switches so that the trains would make new evolutions.

The cops discreetly withdrew, and I resumed consideration of Ligny and his lake. Maybe he was a Thoreau votary and in his travels had made a pilgrimage to Concord, Massachusetts, had tramped around Walden Pond in Thoreau's footsteps and sheltered in the hut Thoreau had built, and this little lake was a tribute to the master.

Then I thought of the stolen book in my pocket. I couldn't take it out to examine it, not here where policemen could watch, but I could visualize the dark red covers and the portrait of Thoreau and the pages of fine, clear print. The pages did not bear the stigmata of long and loving study. And that reminded me that on my first looking into it, the pages had been stiff and inclined to stick together as though they had been undisturbed for years.

Yet Ligny did know something of *Walden*. I recalled that on one occasion when I was talking to him about my caravan, he had called me a "peripatetic Minerva." Later on, I had found the reference in *my* copy of *Walden,* a complaint against Minerva that she had not made her home movable, by which means a bad neighborhood might be avoided.

Again I was in a dead-end street, which caused common sense to renew its clamor. You're a fool, Carmichael; you and your clever reasoning, building imaginary mountains out of nonexistent molehills. Ligny might be food for crabs at Batemans Bay, he might be fleeing with the Law hard on his heels; but so what? There's no profit in scraping the skin off *your* nose.

I heard Stella's voice calling me through the wind. I snarled in self-disgust, switched off the trains and the lamps and obeyed my sister's summons to morning tea.

2

I had confirmation very quickly that my scrap of paper was the sole reason for my being hauled to Canberra. Edmund Martin swallowed a cup of tea, told me he was honored by meeting me, nodded all round and departed with every sign of haste. So that was that.

More leisurely, Stella, Dan and I drank our tea and ate buttered scones and then adjourned to their handsome home next door, leaving the housekeeper and the policemen in charge of Ligny's place. In his den, Dan put in front of me a blank official form headed "Commonwealth of Australia— L2A—Contingencies."

"Your claim for traveling expenses, laddie," Dan said. "Sign at the bottom—where it says 'Claimant.' I'll fill in the details myself. A check will arrive in due course."

"Thank you humbly," I said.

We had lunch, and then Stella and Dan drove me out to the airport. On the way we talked little other than about the foul weather, but just before the PA announced the departure of my flight, I made a final attempt to breach the wall of silence.

"Well," I said to Dan, "did you and Mr. Martin decide it was Ligny's handwriting?"

Dan regarded me with a half-quizzical, half-deprecatory smile.

"It's no use asking me that," he said. "Ted Martin's the man to ask."

"Who is Mr. Martin anyway?" I asked. "Second assistant vice-deputy secretary to the acting Prime Minister's tipstaff or what?"

Dan abandoned his smile.

"Ted Martin is an officer attached to my department," he said. "And here's a piece of advice, laddie. Don't go round talking about what you did and saw today—and last night's incident either. In fact, you should forget you ever knew a man called Ligny."

And I fancy that with common sense once more orating loudly in my mind, I might have heeded Dan's warning but for the reception that greeted me on my arrival at my motel in Parkville. It was a rough flight back to Melbourne and the drive in from Essendon Airport was miserably wet and cold, so that when I opened the door of my motel suite my main consideration was getting hot food into me.

What I did get was a blackjack on my head. Or, maybe, a waddy or a golf club or a man's massive fist. It didn't make any difference. I was out of it for five or ten minutes and I woke up with a diabolical headache. I crouched on the floor until I realized I was not bleeding to death, that, in fact, I wasn't bleeding at all. Then I searched for aspirin tablets, washed four of them down with whiskey and lowered myself onto the bed to wait for the pain to subside.

A quarter of an hour elapsed before I felt fit enough to start investigations. My suite was the usual motel accommodation provided for a single lodger, comprising the bedroom, a short passage leading to the outer door, and the bathroom entered from the passage. It did not take me long to discover that apart from the lump on my head, the intruder had left no trace of his visit other than a quick search. Not a thing had been taken from my cases or the drawers in the dressing table, and although my pockets had obviously been examined, their contents were intact. Wallet, papers, money, the copy of *Walden*—all were safe.

So what had he been after? I went along the passage, opened the door and looked out onto the rain-swept parking area. The security lamps transmuted the sleet into slanting glittering spears. One car was moving out under the portal archway, another was edging in; five or six people were hurrying toward the restaurant beside the entrance.

Nobody took any notice of me. I retreated into the bedroom and scrutinized the window opposite the passage. The window looked out onto a low brick wall, beyond which was a rain-shrouded building that could have been an apartment house. I judged the window was the intruder's probable way of entering, for it was not locked. It had been his way out too. And then the manner of his coming and going did not matter because inspiration had suddenly lighted up his name.

Lewis Ligny—it could only have been Ligny, and this stopped me in my tracks. No yelling for help now, no going howling to the police or motel authorities. How he had managed to locate me I couldn't imagine and I didn't try, but his reason was (to my mind) startlingly clear. He had wanted to retrieve the note we had exchanged in Festival Hall, the scrap of paper I had given to Mr. Martin.

I lay down on the bed to think out my next move, but my head was still throbbing, and moreover, I had become aware of an aching regret. I found myself recalling the appeal (for help, sympathy, forgiveness?) lurking behind Ligny's fierce blue eyes. If only he had spoken to me at Festival Hall, if only he had faced me a few minutes ago instead of knocking me out, I might have made him understand I was a friend. A friend, no matter what dreadful mess he had got himself into at Batemans Bay.

Then common sense started scoffing. What a pretty fantasy

23

of make-believe sentiment, Carmichael! Ligny's in a bad jam; don't get into it yourself. But common sense did not convince me that it was not Ligny who had raided my room.

Thoroughly dissatisfied with Sandy Carmichael, I levered myself off the bed, washed my face and hands, went to the restaurant and made myself eat. After that, I returned to the suite, swallowed more aspirin, crept into bed and slept dreamlessly for ten hours.

The weather maintained its miserable onslaught next day. On wet Sundays, Melbourne is no place for enjoyment, and therefore I confined myself to the motel. Apart from meals in the restaurant, I spent the time in my room examining the stolen *Walden*.

I started by turning to page 300 and studying Thoreau's plan of Walden Pond. With its Merino-like outline bolstering up my memory, I visualized Ligny's lake and its cliffs, bays, surrounding hills and valleys. Ignoring the ports and mines and railroads, I magnified the lake mentally into an actual physical scene, and with the mind's eye seeking one vantage point after another, I pictured various vistas so that (I hoped) I would always recognize them no matter from what direction I approached the genuine region.

More make-believe, common sense said; yet I was rather pleased with this effort, and I embarked optimistically on the next phase—the scrutiny of the text. Somewhere in these rarely touched pages I would come upon words and phrases and paragraphs that would interpret the riddle of Ligny's lake.

But it did not turn out that way. I heard only the robust voice of Thoreau, and finishing the last page late in the afternoon, I was no better off than at the start. Disappointed, I aimlessly turned the leaves back to the beginning. Wishing for a mite of Henry D. Thoreau's transcendental vision, I spent a minute looking at his tissue-guarded portrait and at the disfiguring childish signature of Wesley Griffon Hancock.

I hoped the young Hancock had been suitably punished.

Finally I eyed the bookplate inside the front cover and then it seemed that a pale reflection of Thoreau's inspiration did light on me.

The bookplate read:

Suaviter in modo, fortiter in re

WORRIONG COLLEGE
WORRIONG

Mr. Kelly's Special
Essay Prize
Rhoda Hancock
Christmas, 1900

Worriong College was the real start. It had been the start of this book which I had pinched from Ligny's shelves, and it would be the start of my pilgrimage in Ligny's footsteps, and I had two names for passwords—Mr. Kelly and Rhoda Hancock.

A little after nine o'clock Monday morning I drove into the grounds of Worriong College for Young Ladies (so the sign at the gates said) just in time to see a procession of burgundy-uniformed girls, small and big, march into the assembly. With them were their teachers and also a sprinkling of well-dressed grown-ups, mostly women.

In the office, I presented my card to a bespectacled girl at the inquiries desk and requested an interview with Miss Branchflower, the principal.

The girl frowned and said I had chosen a difficult moment to call. Was I a salesman?

"No," I said. "I'm merely seeking information."

In a manner implying I should have known better, the girl said that the third Monday in August was Founders' Day at Worriong College; Miss Branchflower would be occupied for the next hour with the commemoration ceremonies and of course she mustn't be interrupted. Mr. Carmichael could wait if he liked, or he could return at a more convenient time.

Electing to wait, I retired outside to a sunny corner, for the weather had improved gratifyingly. I lit my pipe, listened to the choir in the assembly hall and surveyed the scene. The college was in a pleasant part of the Victorian Midlands. Worriong Township was a short way down the highway. A couple of leagues eastward was the truncated cone of Mount Worriong, where, some ten million years ago or so, a stupendous Roman candle had pumped out fire and brimstone. But time had softened the volcano's harsh outlines and refined its tuffs and lava flows into dales rich with grass fit for sheep and cattle.

A somnolent place, the right place for a school for carefully nurtured girls. I wondered about Rhoda Hancock, who had been a pupil of note at the turn of the century. I wondered what kind of child she had been and speculated on what she had become. It was fruitless thinking. In all probability her future of 1900 had ended long since in a graveyard and all I should learn of her was that she had once won a special essay prize donated by a Mr. Kelly. But her prize could point the way to Lewis Ligny.

The hour of waiting passed, the choir sang "Nunc Dimittus," the girls in their red uniforms dispersed to classrooms and the old pupils and their menfolk stood in the quadrangle to gossip and laugh before making their way to their cars. Three people, two women and a surpliced clergyman, went by, giving me incurious glances. The cleric was apparently the school chaplain, and I surmised that the square, determined woman in mortarboard and academic robes was Miss Branchflower. As for the second woman, I supposed she was one of the former pupils. She was old but erect and vigorous. Her hair was remarkably white, her complexion pink-gold, her eyes large and bright and very dark; and her furs and clothes signified money and position. The chaplain and the principal escorted her to a venerable Daimler, and she drove down the avenue and out onto the road with a supreme but unconscious air of competence in dealing with either humans or machines.

A genuine *grande dame.*

Miss Branchflower and the chaplain retreated into the office. I waited a decent interval, then followed them.

"Oh, yes," said the girl at the inquiries desk. "Miss Branchflower will see you now."

She shepherded me into a large, high room of steel cabinets and wide glass-fronted bookcases and portraits of past headmistresses. The present incumbent, who had shed her academic trappings, was sitting at her desk, looking at my card.

"Do sit down, Mr. Carmichael," she said in a no-nonsense tone of voice. "I hope you're not trying to sell me something."

I seated myself, glad that in front of Miss Branchflower's impregnable chin, I was no salesman.

"No," I said. "As I told the young lady in the outer office, I'm only after information." I took out Ligny's copy of *Walden* and placed the book on the desk, opened at the bookplate. "I'm seeking information about a certain Mr. Kelly and a certain Rhoda Hancock. As you see, the bookplate has the authority of Worriong College."

Miss Branchflower looked at the bookplate. She gave me a rather startled glance.

"May I ask how you came to get this?" she said.

I had expected the question and was prepared for it in some degree. I didn't like telling a deliberate lie, yet I couldn't confess to stealing the book, so (very conscious of Miss Branchflower's direct gaze) I explained that an acquaintance of mine had found it necessary to relinquish his collection of books and I had seized (the right word) the opportunity to get his copy of *Walden* for myself.

"I'm fond of Thoreau," I said. "But you can understand my surprise at finding the Worriong College bookplate inside the cover."

Miss Branchflower was pensive. "Was your acquaintance a Melbourne book collector?" she asked.

"No, a Canberra man," I said without thinking.

"Very interesting," said Miss Branchflower. "That a book presented to a Worriong pupil in 1900 should return to the school sixty-nine years after, and from Canberra—most interesting. And curious."

"I can see that, Miss Branchflower."

"And in such fine condition, too, except"—Miss Branchflower frowned at the signature of Wesley Griffon Hancock— "for a small boy's mark. But whatever has happened to it in sixty-nine years, it's been taken care of."

"I'd like to know its history," I said. "That is why I've come to you."

"Your friend the collector—didn't he volunteer any information about the book? Where he got it and how and so on?"

"He was an acquaintance merely," I said, feeling like a Judas.

"But you could go to him now and ask him."

"He's left Canberra—traveling, I believe," I said. I was in murky water, and the sooner I got out of it the safer. I went on: "What can you tell me about this Mr. Kelly and Rhoda Hancock, Miss Branchflower?"

"You know," Miss Branchflower said drily, "your coming here on Founders' Day is a coincidence. Mr. Robert Kelly, a local pastoralist, long dead of course, was one of the foundation members of the school council. Now"—Miss Branchflower assumed a tutorial mien—"the school has established a number of worthy traditions. One was initiated by Mr. Kelly. A lover of pure English, he set up an annual award that was to become known as Mr. Kelly's Special Essay Prize. It is given at the Christmas speech night to the pupil who, in the opinion of principal and staff, has written the best essay in prose or verse during the current year. Our school, Mr. Carmichael, has always been recognized by its high standard of English, and Mr. Kelly's special has contributed to that excellence in no mean way."

Well, I thought, I had asked for it. I nodded respectfully.

"The honor is greatly sought after," Miss Branchflower continued. "And as you would imagine, the winner usually comes from the senior forms—the sixteen- and seventeen-year-olds. But—"

Miss Branchflower stood up, and I went to stand too.

"Please don't move, Mr. Carmichael," Miss Branchflower said. "I was about to say that one year the award was gained by a twelve-year-old, the youngest winner in the history of the school. Excuse me . . ."

She went to one of the bookcases, slid back the glass door and pointed at long rows of black leather-bound folios.

"There," she said. "All the prize essays since the school began. A unique symposium of the best thoughts of young girls. And a unique memorial to a farseeing man."

She selected one of the folios, brought it to the desk and put it in front of me. Embossed in gold, the legend on the cover read:

Mr. Kelly's Special Prize Essay
1900
Rhoda Hancock, Form E2

"That's what you wanted, Mr. Carmichael," Miss Branchflower said. "I'll leave you to read in quietness."

I looked hard at Miss Branchflower as she went to the door. If she was smiling, I wasn't able to detect it.

Two and a half thousand words written by a childish hand in faded ink on both sides of yellowing foolscap. I ploughed through the record of the thoughts (as imagined by Rhoda Hancock more than two millennia after the event) of Horatius as he was engaged in keeping the bridge. A precocious young miss, Rhoda, I decided, especially when I read her final sentence that cunningly tied up Horatius' heroic behavior with the school's motto, *Suaviter in modo, fortiter in re—gentle in manner, strong in performance,* indeed! But as for Lewis

Ligny, Rhoda's juvenile rhetorics were as useful as an empty beer can in a dust storm.

Miss Branchflower, judging her time nicely, came in just as I was closing the folio.

"Well, Mr. Carmichael," she said, "what do you think of it?"

"Fascinating," I said. "Though not exactly what I was looking for. But," I hastened to add, "Rhoda Hancock was an able writer for one so young."

"Perhaps the writer herself would prove equally fascinating?"

I stared. There was still no smile on Miss Branchflower's formidable countenance.

"I suppose," she said, "Miss Hancock hasn't missed a Founders' Day ceremony in seventy-five years. You have seen her, Mr. Carmichael—the white-haired lady in the old Daimler. While you were reading her essay, I took the liberty of telephoning her about you."

"The deuce!" I said. Learning that Rhoda Hancock still existed was a sufficient surprise in itself, but Miss Branchflower's ambuscade had the flavor of low cunning. "What was the outcome of the telephone call?" I asked coldly.

"Miss Hancock would like you to go out to her home—immediately if you could," Miss Branchflower said. "She wants to see the book she lost so many years ago. . . ."

Miss Rhoda Hancock's home, Worriong Cottage, was five and a half miles east from the school, sunning itself in a niche on the western slope of Mount Worriong. I drove in from the road between brick pillars, pulled up before a creeper-wreathed porch and looked at the peaceful old house, at the trees and gardens and up at the scoriaceous outcrops of the lifeless volcano. This is it, I thought, the place you really go after Ligny or forget all about him. Either way, get it over and done with.

The front door was open. As I stepped onto the porch, a plump, blue-eyed, middle-aged woman appeared.

"Mr. Carmichael?" she said. "I'm Mrs. Riley, Miss Hancock's housekeeper. Do come in."

I thanked her and entered an old-fashioned hall. I saw a staircase rising to the top floor, and four doors, one on the left, two on the right and one beside the stairs opposite the front door.

Mrs. Riley conducted me to the door on the left and into a large formal drawing room and onto a recess or bay almost as large. This alcove was clearly a favored resort. The chairs had a look of well-worn comfort, the blackwood table held newspapers and magazines and cigarettes, the bookshelves were handy to the chairs; and through the two wide windows, there was a view of the west Midland country curving around to the horizon of the northern plains beyond Mount Worriong's steep flanks.

The housekeeper said, "This is Mr. Carmichael, Miss Hancock."

Like Agag, I went into the alcove delicately. Miss Hancock stood up and regarded me for a few seconds without speaking. She had changed from her furs and costume of her attendance at Founders' Day into something less imposing, but I was conscious only of her white hair and pink-gold skin and dark eyes. Eighty-one? Good Lord! I was suddenly nervous, afraid of being hewed into pieces in Miss Hancock's opinion.

She pointed to a chair. "Sit down, Mr. Carmichael, please."

Her voice was calm, clear, low-pitched, neither friendly nor hostile. We took our seats, and the chair Miss Hancock indicated for me had me facing the strong light of the north window. Mrs. Riley departed by a side door, which was allowed to remain open. Precaution, I told myself.

"I'm told you have a book that belongs to me," Miss Hancock said.

"Yes, Miss Hancock, and here it is."

I got out the red-covered copy of *Walden* and gave it to Miss Hancock, again opened at the bookplate. Miss Hancock put on a pair of rimless spectacles.

31

"Well!" she said. She held the book in both hands. "Well!" she repeated. She riffled through the pages, then returned to Thoreau's portrait. "There's young Wesley's name," she said. "It really is my Thoreau. After all these years! Just look here, Mr. Carmichael."

Miss Hancock turned in her chair and touched four books in the shelf nearby, all of the same size and red binding and format, and all uniform with *Walden*.

"There's the rest of my essay prize," she said. "Emerson's *Nature*, his *Early Poems*, his *English Traits* and Souvestre's *Attic Philosopher*. The gap for *Walden* has been empty for twenty-eight years and I never thought to see it filled again. You must excuse my excitement, Mr. Carmichael, but after all this time. . . . I must confess when Miss Branchflower telephoned, I was inclined to think—"

She paused, a friendly gleam in her eyes. Perhaps there was justifiable reason for Miss Branchflower's Machiavellian game; at any rate, I finished Miss Hancock's thought for her.

"Was inclined to think," I said, "a con man was working one of his schemes."

"I admit the thought did arise," Miss Hancock said. "But this is my Thoreau. Mr. Carmichael, how did you get— But I'm forgetting my manners."

I can only assume the housekeeper picked up a signal to the effect the visitor was trustworthy or at least not dangerous, for she came in wheeling a tray of tea and cakes and scones. Miss Hancock took off her glasses.

"Milk and sugar?" she asked, pouring tea.

"Yes, thank you. One teaspoonful, please."

"A scone?"

"Yes, please."

These dispositions organized, the housekeeper retired and Miss Hancock said, "And now, Mr. Carmichael, how did my *Walden* get into your possession?"

I looked into Miss Hancock's magnificent eyes. There could be no shilly-shallying with this old lady, no devious skidding around facts as with Miss Branchflower. For Miss Hancock the whole story of Ligny (as I knew it) had to come out.

"I stole it, Miss Hancock," I said.

"*You* stole my Thoreau!"

"Yes, Miss Hancock, and I'm going to tell you how I came to steal it, and I hope I get your understanding of my motive. But first, would you mind telling me how you lost the book?"

"Very well," she said, "though there's not much to say. The five books stood for many years in their place." She pointed at the four companion volumes to *Walden*. "I can remember one day seeing the five books there. The next time I looked at them two or three days later, *Walden* had gone. And that is all I can say. Though I might have had suspicions, I really don't know more than that, except— Mr. Carmichael, how old are you?"

"Twenty-nine."

"Then it's most unlikely you were the original thief. And now for your story, Mr. Carmichael."

I began by relating how and when I first met Lewis Ligny and what I had learned of him, and I described his marred face and his den and the engineering model in his annex. Then I told of his disappearance at Batemans Bay, of my seeing him at Festival Hall, of my rush trip to Canberra next day, of the intruder in my motel suite, of my studying *Walden* yesterday and of the reasons for my coming to Worriong Cottage.

"Strange," Miss Hancock said at the end of the recital. "So strange I'd have shown you the door but for two things. One is, I read about Mr. Ligny's disappearance in Saturday's paper. The other— But there's no time for that just now. Here's Mrs. Riley to call us in to lunch."

It would seem that Worriong Cottage had accepted me. . . .

3

We took lunch in the dining room alongside the alcove. Here I met Herbert Riley, the husband of Miss Hancock's house-keeper. A taciturn man, Mr. Riley, but Miss Hancock informed me he was foreman of the Hancock Stud Sheep Estate, the domain of which Worriong Cottage had once formed part. If Mr. Carmichael cared to look through the window, he would glimpse three miles away the Worriong homestead and some of the many acres the Hancocks used to own.

Then Miss Hancock went on to talk about the Hancocks. For instance, her grandfather William Hancock. William and the Mr. Robert Kelly of Special Essay Prize fame had been the pioneers of the Worriong district and had divided many square miles of choice country between themselves.

Then there was Miss Hancock's father, Walter, in whose reign had begun the squatters' disgorging much of their land for closer settlement. There was also Miss Hancock's Uncle Mick, an eccentric recluse who had spent his days in a hut on the other side of Mount Worriong. Finally, there were Miss Hancock's brother Quentin, his wife, Royena, their son, Wesley (the same who had defaced Thoreau's portrait) and their daughter, Elspeth, with whom Miss Hancock had lived at the old homestead until the Second War started and the army appropriated the homestead for its own peculiar purposes. The Hancocks had then taken up residence in Worriong Cottage with the exception of Wesley, also an eccentric, who enlisted in the army and marched off to war and died.

The Hancocks had quickly suffered another casualty in Elspeth, though not as a result of warfare; leukemia was the cause of her death. The remaining Hancocks lived quietly at Worriong Cottage until the war had ended, and then Quentin and Royena returned to the homestead. However, Miss Hancock, wanting to be independent, decided to stay on at the cottage. In a way, that decision had been wise, for Quentin and Royena had been fatally injured in a car accident soon after their return to the homestead. Because of the heavy death duties and not willing to run a large sheep run, Miss Hancock had disposed of the estate to a pastoral company, retaining only Worriong Cottage as her home. And here she still was, she said, very fortunate in her old age.

I wondered why she was telling me all this. I discovered the reason after lunch when Mr. Riley had gone back to his job at the homestead and Miss Hancock and I had returned to the alcove. Miss Hancock invited me to smoke; then she opened a drawer holding a stack of black-covered exercise books. She sorted through these, picked one out and put it on the table.

She sat for a while steadily regarding me, and I was conscious again of her black glowing eyes and erect back and white hair and golden skin.

"Mr. Carmichael," she began, "I told you I would have shown you the door but for two things. One was the announcement of Mr. Ligny's disappearance. The other is this." She touched the exercise book. "No doubt you've gathered the Hancocks have been an eccentric family. I'm no better than the rest. For many years, I have kept double diaries—

more precisely, two streams of diaries. In one series, I record facts, happenings, events—quite objectively. In the other series, I record my private candid thoughts, feelings, reactions to people and events.

"I've also developed another quirk, Mr. Carmichael. In the objective series, I don't mix up events. Each book deals strictly with one event only and its relevant facts. This"— Miss Hancock indicated the book on the table—"belongs to the objective series and there are a lot of empty pages in it— You're surprised, Mr. Carmichael?"

"Yes," I said. "And I'm also wondering which series *I'll* be appearing in."

"You're laughing at me, Mr. Carmichael."

"I'm not laughing, Miss Hancock. I would honestly like to know what you think of me."

"I'll tell you what I think later on," said Miss Hancock. "In the meantime, there's a second explanation. At lunch, I talked about my family. I wasn't showing off, trying to impress you, though it might have sounded like that. When you read what I've written in this book, you'll see you couldn't have understood what was happening without knowing something about the Hancocks."

"Thank you, Miss Hancock."

"One more thing—a question," she said. "This mysterious Mr. Ligny, the vanishing man, the man who shammed a drowning at Batemans Bay, the man who could have attacked you in the motel—are you really motivated by a liking for him, or are you merely prying?"

I comprehended that Miss Hancock was making a last test of whether I was a cheat or not.

"I liked Lewis Ligny," I said, "and I still do. Whatever his trouble, if I can help him, I certainly will."

"Strange," said Miss Hancock, "but I believe you. Well, there's the diary. You can read that, and I'll start renewing my acquaintance with Henry David Thoreau."

Adjusting her spectacles, she settled back in her chair with

36

Walden in her hand, and I relit my pipe and opened the black-covered exercise book. I spent some moments comparing the swift mature handwriting of the first page with the schoolgirl script of the essay in Miss Branchflower's office. But I was no expert in calligraphy, and I couldn't find any indication that the same writer had penned diary and composition, and so I got to work with my reading. The diary started without preamble.

Monday, 8 Sept., '41

Four new soldiers arrived 9 A.M. to take up residence in the homestead. When we gathered in the sunroom for morning tea, I mentioned the arrivals, speaking of them as "four officers." Elspeth laughed and said, "You don't know much about the army, Aunt Rhoda. They are not all officers. One's a captain, one's a warrant officer and two are sergeants."

Royena said it didn't matter if they were generals or privates, the Hancocks would have to entertain them, and it would be a good thing when the war was over, and Elspeth laughed again.

I suspect Elspeth has had a closer look at the newcomers than I had. My binoculars aren't exactly where I had left them.

I looked up from the diary, excused myself and asked Miss Hancock where the sunroom was.

"Right here," Miss Hancock said. "You're in it now. We always call it the sunroom."

And with the sunlight pouring in on me through the west window, I could understand.

Tuesday, 9 Sept., '41

Horribly wet and cold, so Royena, Elspeth and I stayed indoors, but it seems our new soldiers are not here for rest and recreation like previous guests. At lunch Quentin announced a lot of the run has been declared out of bounds to civilians. He had measurements and specifications which I can't understand, but it boils down to that the north and west sides of Mount Worriong with about two miles of country around are verboten.

Royena, again complaining against the war, wanted to know why.

37

"Don't know," said Quentin. "I was only talking to an orderly and he didn't tell me why. All I know is I've got to shift all the stock from those paddocks. And while I'm talking about it, the army would like you to keep out of the crater itself."

"Why the crater?" I asked.

"If you go into the crater, you might be tempted to climb the scarp and peep over the other side," said Elspeth.

Something to think about.

Thursday, 11 Sept., '41

At lunch today, Quentin announced that at dinner tomorrow evening the Hancocks would be entertaining the new arrivals in the well-known Hancock style.

Royena groaned to high heaven. Elspeth expressed excitement. I merely felt faintly curious.

Friday, 12 Sept., '41

I climbed into the crater this morning to get a basket of golden wattle—the wattle in the crater is always better and lasts longer than outside where the wind batters it.

After filling the basket, I yielded to temptation and went up the northwest scarp—there are thick scrubby trees there to make good cover. I didn't see much, only four tiny figures running across the paddocks far below. Next time—if there is a next time—I'll take my binoculars with me.

Our guests arrived at six-thirty and filed into the drawing room, and I realized Elspeth had *not* observed them earlier as closely as I thought. All Hancocks have been schooled in the social code—in the Hancock code, at least. We did not stare.

The visitors are all young, all big and all (despite the initial awkward pause) look strangely alike with brown or reddish hair and blue or gray eyes. The battle dress uniform helped this illusion, but the chief reason for their similarity is their still expression and the lean look of their faces conveying an air of extreme physical fitness combined with extreme mental rigor.

Their uniforms (at least the dress they wore tonight) are devoid of badges except the insignia of rank. No unit tabs, no ribbons, no chevrons indicating they had served overseas. And their berets had a deep purple color I had not seen before.

Royena, Elspeth and I stood up when Quentin rather stumblingly introduced our guests.

First, Captain Lewis Ligny—

Lewis Ligny! A sudden excitement blazed through me. I lowered the exercise book and looked at Miss Hancock, but she was apparently engrossed in Thoreau and didn't evince any sign of having noticed my start. I returned to the diary.

—second, Warrant Officer Hugh Martin, then Sergeant Wilfrid Giles and last, Sergeant Garrett Blair. We shook hands and then Elspeth and I handed—

I stopped again and went back to the second name, W.O. Hugh Martin. Martin? But the Canberra Mr. Martin's first name was Edmund, and he wasn't old enough to have been a Second War veteran. Besides, his thick tousled look was nothing like the big, lean, ascetic type Miss Hancock had described. Yet the juxtaposition of Ligny and Martin was certainly strange.

—around sherry. There was some courteous conversation, then we went into the dining room. Dinner was pleasant, the wine good, and the talk livened up to the extent we got on to first name terms. They addressed me as "Aunt Rhoda." It was Sergeant Giles who started *that* practice, but there was no mention of war and no hint of what these four soldiers were doing at Mount Worriong.

We went back to the drawing room, Quentin dispensed whiskey, and Sergeant Giles sat down at the piano and played Schubert for a while, and the others circulated among the Hancocks and talked. At nine o'clock, Captain Ligny looked at his watch and said, "Lights Out at twenty-one thirty, men." Thereupon, they thanked us civilly for an enjoyable evening, donned their purple berets, saluted smartly, piled into their jeep and departed.

We sat down to review the function in silence. I would only guess at the thoughts of Quentin, Royena and Elspeth, but as for myself, I thought of two remarks, both made by Sergeant Giles in the course of the evening.

The first: "Aunt Rhoda, your niece is so like you, especially about the eyes. You and Elspeth are versions of the same beautiful flower"—an acceptably elegant compliment but for the gleam in his blue eyes.

The second: Quentin said to Captain Ligny, "I see you men don't wear shoulder tabs. What exactly are you?"

"Sappers," said Captain Ligny.

And beside me, whispering to himself, Sergeant Giles said so softly I couldn't have heard it but my extra-sharp hearing, "Suckers, you mean, you swine."

I deduced that Sergeant Giles did not like his commanding officer.

I put down the diary and glanced at its compiler. Miss Hancock had just turned over a page of *Walden*. I recalled Thoreau's puzzling dictum about the ladies of the land weaving toilet cushions against the last day. Had Miss Hancock spent her eighty-one years weaving cushions? At any rate, Sergeant Giles, if he were here again, could still regard Miss Hancock as a version of a beautiful flower and this time mean it. I started to read again.

Sunday, 14 Sept., '41

This morning we went to church in Worriong, and to our surprise, Capt. Ligny, W.O. Martin and Sgts. Giles and Blair were among the worshipers.

We were more surprised when W.O. Martin and Sgts. Giles and Blair came to the cottage in the afternoon. They apologized for the unexpected intrusion, but having some free time, they had started out for a walk and, when they came to the cottage, they couldn't resist popping in.

We asked where was Capt. Ligny? Up to his eyes in paper work, they said. Quentin offered sherry and whiskey, which they politely declined. Elspeth wanted to make tea, but again they declined. They would be staying only a few minutes and then on again.

The few minutes became more like three hours. Out of Capt. Ligny's sight, they were like schoolboys on holiday. They played the piano, they rummaged through my books in the sunroom, they wandered in the garden and paid court to Elspeth. Then Sgt. Blair uttered a hoot of dismay. "Quarter to five! Oh, God, The Trump! And we've got three miles to cover!"

There were hurried farewells; then they went doubling down

the road, their heavy army boots clop-clop-clopping in the still cold air. There would be a white frost tonight, I thought.

"What's The Trump?" asked Elspeth.

"Who, you mean," said Quentin. "Capt. Ligny's The Trump, and even if they run four-minute miles, they'll be A.W.O.L."

"I hate Capt. Ligny," said Elspeth.

Taking pity, I ran my car out despite the petrol rationing, picked up the defaulters along the road and got them to the homestead with a minute to spare. Then I cleared out of the place before Capt. Ligny could charge me with trespassing on an army establishment.

Monday, 15 Sept., '41

This morning, indulging my penchant to view the sun rising over frosted earth, I was up by six and soon after was climbing the mount. The world was cold and white and hard. The only sounds were my panting breath, the crunching of my shoes on frozen grass and the early caroling of magpies below the cottage.

When I scrambled up the northwest scarp, a dull red glow was forming in the mists swathing the eastern ranges. To the west, the low-lying land was static and pallid and mist lay along the hollows. The homestead was a dark square clump surrounded by white, and I could just glimpse a blue feather of smoke rising from the chimneys of the cottage.

The sun came up, red streaked with brown. It broke clear of the mists and earth, trees, frost, all signaled a myriad diamond points of light in welcome. This is a very ancient human rite, watching the sun rise, and I was about to think profound thoughts when someone began a violent shouting.

I turned sharply and looked down the great smooth sweep of the northwest escarpment. At the bottom were four small figures racing straight up the slope. This time, I had my binoculars with me, and I focused them on the runners—Capt. Ligny, W.O. Martin and Sgts. Giles and Blair, of course.

They ran barefooted and they wore shorts only, and their sun-tanned bodies were dark against the white frost. Through the binoculars I could see their identification badges bobbing from their necks—the "meat tickets," they call them. But it was the look of their faces that caught my attention. The expression of resources, physical, mental, spiritual, drained beyond the last final effort. It was Capt. Ligny who did the shouting. I thought at first he was

41

punishing the others for calling on us yesterday, but he was driving himself just as cruelly. In the still cold, I could hear their shuddering gasps for breath.

The ground lifted under their feet, and their speed slackened, but they came on and up until their progress degenerated into a mad creeping kangaroo kind of gallop on the precipitous grade.

"Down and run!" croaked Capt. Ligny. "Run! Damn you, run!"

He turned, started to run and fell. He rolled eight or ten feet before he could regain his footing. Two of the others also fell, but the fourth by some miracle held his balance and he shot down the hill, striding prodigiously. But his triumph was short-lived. He tripped, somersaulted and went on rolling and threshing for fifty or sixty yards. It was a horrible fall. Through the binoculars, I could see the lacerations on his back and legs, his blood staining the mud he had collected in that last mad plunge.

His companions ran past him, Capt. Ligny cursing him, and he slowly sat up and just as slowly got to his feet and started hobbling after the others, now a quarter of a mile away across the paddock.

I never said a word of what I saw, but at breakfast Quentin spoke portentously.

"I suspect you were on the mount this morning. Well, you won't be able to say you weren't warned when Capt. Ligny takes action. But you won't be the victim of his oppression. Someone else will have to bear the brunt of it."

I did not debate the point.

I looked up from the diary. Miss Hancock, deserting Thoreau for a moment, was lighting a cigarette.

"Anything worrying you?" she asked.

"Just a question," I said. "I've been reading your description of the four men racing up the mount. Who was the man who fell, Miss Hancock?"

"Now that's odd," she said. "I really don't know. I could see them coming up the mount, could pick each out in the binoculars, but in the confusion of turning and slipping— they all had falls—I missed who had the bad fall. I do know it was not Captain Ligny; he was the one who did the shouting."

"But later on, Miss Hancock, you could have picked the

injured man by his—well—his battle wounds. He must have been hurt."

"He *was* hurt, Mr. Carmichael, but I didn't see the men for about a fortnight, as the diary will show, and by then his scars had disappeared."

"I see."

"But I have a question myself," Miss Hancock said. "What was the purpose— No, I'll let it wait till you've read about the unarmed combat, and that's quite a while to go."

Miss Hancock and I returned to our respective books.

I skimmed the next two pages quickly, for they contained dates under which appeared remarks like "No entry" or "Nothing to report," the dates that covered the fortnight during which Miss Hancock had not seen the soldiers at the homestead. Then the diary resumed its initial swing and zest.

Tuesday, 30 Sept., '41

Today, Elspeth and I lighted on a fascinating though puzzling scene. Left alone at home because Quentin had taken Royena to Ballarat for a medical check, and the weather being superlatively fine, we decided to walk to Mick's Hollow, a place we hadn't visited for years. We went armed with binoculars, sandwiches and a thermos of tea, and we took the long way around the south and east sides of the Mount to avoid violation of military interdicts.

Mick's Hollow is two miles northeast of the Mount and, by my calculation, well outside martial jurisdiction. But, goodness, we found the army in occupation. Fortunately for Elspeth and me, the army was making a lot of noise, and so we were able to steal unnoticed down through the Chinese scrub and gain a good vantage point without being spotted.

We saw our acquaintances, Capt. Ligny, W.O. Martin and Sgts. Giles and Blair (none of them bearing scars). First I thought they were playing a parlor game, but though there was much talking (mainly from Capt. Ligny, luckily not too profane), they were deadly serious, and I came to the conclusion there was a kind of geography lesson in progress.

On the grassy plat in front of poor old Uncle Mick Hancock's tumbledown hut, they had set up a portable blackboard. In turn, each donned a blindfold, took a piece of chalk and drew a large outline on the blackboard. The idea, seemingly, was to complete the outline where it had started, and I recalled that Miss Fisher, the geography teacher at the college in my day, used to employ the same means to make us remember the shapes of maps. But this was no map—at least, no map of any country I had to draw.

Over and over they went until slowly they achieved a measure of success. Then Capt. Ligny introduced a new development. Each man in turn had to run at full speed around the hollow until he was gasping and then, blindfolded and still shaking for breath, had to try and draw the outline again.

This procedure was a failure, and now Capt. Ligny did use horrifying language. After a while, he cooled down and the four men discussed the results, but in such cryptic technical terms Elspeth and I couldn't get any idea of what the exercise was for. Finally they stowed blackboard, easel and chalk inside Uncle Mick's hut and departed at a hard double in the direction of the homestead.

"Well, what was all that about?" said Elspeth.

"Heaven knows," I said.

We climbed up out of the hollow, found a sunny spot and sat down to eat our sandwiches and drink our tea.

"I know who could tell us," Elspeth said.

"I know, too," I said. "But we won't ask him."

"Why?"

"How many men have they got at the homestead?" I asked. "Cooks, batmen, orderlies or whatever they call them?"

"Nine," said Elspeth, "according to Father."

"Well, Elspeth, the antics we've witnessed, whatever they mean, are something secret, so secret the staff at the homestead mustn't see them."

"I don't understand."

"Goodness, Elspeth! All this blindfold exercising could have been done much more comfortably at the homestead. Instead, Capt. Ligny and his men had to come out here to Uncle Mick's hut, forgotten for years."

"Oh, I see," said Elspeth.

"So," I told her, "no word about this to anyone, even to your father and mother."

And that was that, but tonight in my bedroom, after six or seven feeble attempts, I have just drawn with eyes shut the outline we saw in Mick's Hollow.

"Excuse me, Miss Hancock."

"Yes, Mr. Carmichael?"

"Two queries. I've just read your entry of Tuesday, 30 September, 1941—the account of the 'antics' in Mick's Hollow. Was it Sergeant Giles your niece had in mind to ask for an explanation?"

"Quite correct, Mr. Carmichael."

"The second query, Miss Hancock. Can you recall the outline the men were trying to draw?"

"I can do better than that, Mr. Carmichael. I kept my copy of the outline. You'll find it toward the back of the diary among the empty pages."

I switched the leaves over until I found a loose sheet of white drawing paper. Though the outline I saw on the paper was not an accurate reproduction of the shape of Ligny's lake, it was near enough, and I said, "Miss Hancock, would you please look at page 300 of *Walden*?"

She did so, and her dark eyes grew intense as she looked at Thoreau's plan of Walden Pond, drawn in 1846.

"Goodness me!" she said. "I'd forgotten this."

4

Miss Hancock again chose to defer discussion and speculation until I had completed reading the diary. The time was only two o'clock, she said; it would take me ten or twelve minutes at the most to read the rest of the diary, and then we would have a cup of coffee and settle down to analyze the whole problem.

So, displaying a facile power of concentration, Miss Hancock returned to Thoreau, and I, less able to control my thinking, found the place in the diary where I had left off.

Thursday, 2 Oct., '41

I have been back to Mick's Hollow this morning, alone this time because Elspeth is unwell. But I have told her what I saw, and in its way it was quite as interesting as Tuesday.

Our military friends held a modeling seance. All four, Capt. Ligny, the W.O. and the two sergeants, sat on campstools, balanced boards on their knees and kneaded blue plasticine onto the boards.

They worked in silence for most of the time. At the end, they stood their boards against the front wall of Uncle Mick's hut, then stood back to examine their handiwork.

I looked at the models through my binoculars, and I could see they had each fashioned an outline just like the outline they had drawn on the blackboard. If I had been asked, I would have said they had modeled a deformed sheep—a starving sheep because of the ridgelike ribs carved into the body.

They had a brief discussion, then they stripped the plasticine off the boards and started over again, but now they were blindfolded. They would have looked comical except for their grim air of urgency. Whatever they were up to, it was a serious business.

Again they lined their boards against the wall and examined the results. Capt. Ligny was displeased and he said so. His model was passable, but the others' efforts were deplorable. I hope I never again have to listen to a searing diatribe, but W.O. Martin and Sgts. Giles and Blair merely listened wooden-faced.

In the end, they put the campstools, boards and plasticine away in the hut and, as before, they departed at a hard run for the homestead. But this time, before they went, they chained and padlocked the door, else I might have been tempted to look inside.

Friday, 3 Oct., '41

Quentin, coming in for lunch from the paddocks, reported seeing four men, clad only in shorts, racing up and down the Mount. Obviously Capt. Ligny and his men, he said. He prognosticated sudden death from heart failure for all of them.

Saturday, 4 Oct., '41

10 P.M. Elspeth has just told me she met one of the sergeants this afternoon. How and where, she refused to say, but she did vouchsafe one fact. She asked the sergeant when could the Hancocks expect to entertain our guests again. Never, said the sergeant; Capt. Ligny has placed Worriong Cottage out of bounds to all military personnel.

Monday, 6 Oct., '41

Out at Mick's Hollow this morning, alone again, and another surprising development, or, perhaps, just a continuation of past events, but surprising, all the same.

Capt. Ligny has had heaps of damp creek sand brought in, and he and his troops were spreading the sand in the now well-known one-legged sheep shape. They went on to raise the riblike ridges and added refinements in what could be described as connecting ligaments and tendons.

This completed, each man was blindfolded and disorientated by being led around the hollow several times and by being whirled on his heels, and then he was taken to the edge of the sand formation. He had to creep over and between the ridges without dislodging them, and at the same time, he had to say where he was in relation to the head of the sheep. The technical jargon the men used was meaningless to me but comprehensible to their companions.

This experiment was seemingly satisfactory, for Capt. Ligny, although praising no one, didn't fulminate, and after shoveling the sand out of its original form, they departed in the usual manner.

Tuesday, 7 Oct., '41

A catastrophe today. Elspeth and I went to Mick's Hollow, and long before we could creep down through the scrub, we heard horrid sounds of fighting. Gaining our customary spy seat, we saw two men struggling furiously on the ground (on the sand left yesterday). W.O. Martin and Sgt. Blair stood by the hut watching poker-faced, so the fighters had to be Capt. Ligny and Sgt. Giles.

They fought like animals, slashing, kicking, gouging, all the time uttering bloodcurdling yells. Their shirts were torn to ribbons, and their faces and bodies were bleeding profusely. Elspeth and I sat paralyzed until Capt. Ligny chopped his hand on Sgt. Giles's neck. Sgt. Giles went limp and Capt. Ligny started to throttle him.

At this Elspeth ran down and attacked Capt. Ligny, beating his head with her clenched fists. He turned on her with a roar, stopped, then got up to his feet with such a look of rage I had to appear myself. I believed for a moment he was going to attack Elspeth, who was now down on the sand, cradling Sgt. Giles's head in her lap.

Silence. The eyes of W.O. Martin and Sgt. Blair nearly started out of their heads. More silence. Then Capt. Ligny, striving for breath and forcing his features into a pretense of calm, said, "What are you ladies doing here?"

"You were killing him," Elspeth said.

"You were, too," I said.

"Whether I was killing him or not is irrelevant," Capt. Ligny said. "You have no right to be here."

"Whether or not you have the right to kill a man on army terri-

48

tory," I said, "you're outside the boundaries you laid down your-self. This is Hancock land. You've been trespassing here for days."

"So you've been here before?" said Capt. Ligny.

"Often."

"Lately?"

"Of course."

"Unfortunate," said Capt. Ligny. "Unfortunate, too, that you should witness an advanced lesson in unarmed combat."

"You were killing him," Elspeth said.

Capt. Ligny glanced down at Sgt. Giles, who was showing signs of regaining his wits.

"Stand up, Sergeant."

Despite Elspeth's demurring, Sgt. Giles stood up groggily.

"Just tell these ladies what was going on, Sergeant."

Sgt. Giles spoke through swollen lips.

"Just an exercise in unarmed combat," he said.

The faces of W.O. Martin and Sgt. Blair became even more wooden.

"There you are, ladies," said Capt. Ligny. "War isn't pretty, and we are soldiers and have to train for any set of circumstances, ugly as they might be. So would you mind leaving us to get on with our work."

"Finishing off throttling your victim, of course," said Elspeth. "No, thank you. We're staying here."

"*Our* land, remember," I said.

That was the end of it, though Capt. Ligny tried to expostulate with us. We stayed determinedly put until the soldiers left the field to us; then Elspeth sat down and cried.

P.S. At 5 P.M. I was with Royena in the kitchen and Quentin came in to report he saw our guests departing for parts unknown in an army vehicle laden with kit bags. I went to tell Elspeth of this, and I had to search for her. At length I found her hidden in the garden. She was crying again.

I assumed this was the climax of the diary, but on turning to the next page, I found four more entries, all short, pithy and significant.

Thursday, 4 Dec., '41

In army casualty lists today are the names of W.O. Hugh Martin,

Sgt. Wilfrid Giles and Sgt. Garrett Blair, all killed accidentally. No details given.

Wednesday, 19 May, '42

Today's papers announced Capt. Lewis Ligny has been awarded the George Cross.

Friday, 12 Mar., '48

At the Melbourne University graduation ceremony yesterday, a Mr. Lewis Ligny took out a First Honors degree in Electrical Engineering.

Saturday, 16 Aug., '69

A news item today states a Mr. Lewis Ligny disappeared yesterday, presumably drowned while rockfishing at Batemans Bay.

Right up to date, Miss Hancock, I thought, and then I realized I had been too hasty with that judgment. Miss Hancock must have been watching me, because with a word of apology, she took the diary, found a ballpoint, wrote swiftly and handed the diary back to me.

Now she was really up to date.

Monday, 18 Aug., '69

Today Mr. Carmichael returned my Thoreau, missing for twenty-eight years. He discovered it among the books of the fugitive Mr. Ligny.

This last bald statement rocketed into sight a question that so far I had considered only incidentally. How *did* Miss Hancock's copy of *Walden* get into Ligny's possession? The glib answer was that Ligny himself had stolen it. But I could sense some objections to this. For one thing, according to Miss Hancock's diary, Captain Ligny had had only one opportunity to purloin the book—the occasion of the dinner party—and it could be taken for granted he had been under the eyes of

50

one or other of the Hancocks all the time. And then there were Miss Hancock's own words.

"Miss Hancock," I said, "it looks on the surface that Ligny helped himself to *Walden*. But you told me that when you found the book gone, you might have had suspicions. What suspicions, Miss Hancock?"

"*Might* was the word," said Miss Hancock. "But now we know Captain Ligny was the thief, I don't think we'll go into the matter of my suspicions. I suggest we don't pursue that line any further, Mr. Carmichael."

The object of her suspicions was no doubt recorded in that *other* diary in which she had given rein to her reactions to people and events. I had a quick acute insight into the intensity of her feelings toward Ligny. Momentarily I wished I could read what she had written in that other diary; then I shunned the idea. To amass indictments against Ligny was no part of my purpose. At all costs, I had to believe in him.

I discovered Miss Hancock watching me, her dark eyes bright and inquiring. I placed the diary on the table.

"I've been reading between lines," I said. "You did not like Captain Ligny."

"I hated him," she said calmly. "So did Elspeth, and so did her father and mother. We all detested him from the start. Subsequent events justified us."

"What did you think of the other fellows—Martin, Giles, Blair?"

"I had no complaints against them. Not saints, not sinners, they were normal young men."

"Did you learn anything about their background?"

"They did not volunteer information, Mr. Carmichael, and the Hancocks did not pry."

"Of course, Miss Hancock, Elspeth was in love with Giles."

"If by that you mean the popular connotation of the term —no, she wasn't. And she wasn't in love with Martin or Blair either. The one big emotion was hate for Captain Ligny—on the part of the Hancocks and the part of his men, too."

51

I began to think that after all I would like an opportunity to peruse that other diary. Mrs. Riley brought in the promised cups of coffee. I looked through the north window at the awesome flank of Mount Worriong where four young men had pitted their strength beyond endurance—yes, the other diary was what I wanted, but I could not voice the wish.

Mrs. Riley having retired, I said, "The fight you saw in Mick's Hollow, was it a real fight?"

"I'm not expert in fighting," Miss Hancock said, "but I would say it was. Why?"

"I'm looking—I'm frank, Miss Hancock—for a lifeline for Lewis Ligny. It is possible that what you saw was what Captain Ligny said it was—an exercise in unarmed combat."

"It was a mortal struggle, Mr. Carmichael."

"Was the fight over Elspeth?"

"I've already told you Elspeth was not in love with any of those men. Her running down into the hollow and attacking Captain Ligny was a normal human reaction. You would intervene even if a dog was being beaten to death."

"Does that second diary have the complete description of the fight, Miss Hancock?"

"That diary is my confessional," Miss Hancock said. Her smile had a hint of acid. "I can't share my sins with other people, but I did hate Captain Ligny. From which you may gather I don't consider hating Captain Ligny a sin."

I shook my head. I had to cling to the conviction that Ligny had suffered, and was still suffering, a horrible injustice, and to do that I had to find a way of explaining the old events at Mount Worriong.

"Mr. Carmichael," said Miss Hancock, "this is the question I postponed earlier. Have you had any experience of army life?"

"I served in Vietnam, Miss Hancock."

"You should know what you're talking about, then. We had many soldiers here, before Captain Ligny and his men and after, but only Captain Ligny's party came here to train. All the others were here for rest and recreation. What kind of project could Captain Ligny and his men have been working for? The torturing physical exertion, the blindfold exercises with the sheeplike shape, the secrecy—what did they point to?"

"You've thought about this a lot, Miss Hancock."

"I've had twenty-eight years of thinking, but to no avail. What can you suggest?"

"It was wartime," I said. "It could have been preparing for any one of hundreds of missions. But I'm looking for Ligny himself, not what he did."

"He doesn't want to be found," Miss Hancock said, "and so the nature of the mission is important. We have three factors—Captain Ligny's mutilated face, his winning of the George Cross, the deaths of Hugh Martin, Wilfrid Giles and Garrett Blair. Were these factors generated at the same place and at the same time?"

"I guess the army has the information," I said. "But the army wouldn't divulge that information—to me, at any rate. I have no standing with the army."

"Then look for something that reminds you of a one-legged Merino ewe," said Miss Hancock. She again studied me speculatively. "I'd like to find it myself. I'd like to find Captain Ligny as well. I want to ask him, for instance, why the Hancocks never got word from Hugh Martin or Wilfrid Giles or Garrett Blair after they had gone away from here."

"Was there any reason why you *should* have got word, Miss Hancock?"

"Certainly there was," she said. "Courtesy, for one thing. We entertained lots of soldiers here, and all wrote afterwards thanking us for our hospitality—all except Captain Ligny's men. But there was another reason, an overwhelming reason for expecting word. And it never came."

I waited until it was obvious Miss Hancock would not enlarge on the overwhelming reason. For that I would have to go to the other diary.

"What would Ligny have to do with their not writing?" I asked.

"Everything, Mr. Carmichael. I don't know the present procedure, but in the Second War it was an officer's duty to censor the letters written by his men. No letters came from Captain Ligny's men because he censored their letters out of existence. But we got *his* message in the announcement they had been killed accidentally."

This was more than I had bargained for, more than I was prepared to accept, and Miss Hancock did not fail to observe my fretting.

"Mr. Carmichael," she said, "you remember that at the start I asked you for your motives in looking for your Mr. Ligny, and you said you would help him if you could whatever his trouble. At the time, I expressed surprise."

"I remember, Miss Hancock. And it seems we are now on opposite sides of the fence."

"Well, now, that doesn't inevitably follow." She spent some seconds gazing out at Mount Worriong, where the afternoon tree shadows were creeping up the slope. "Twenty-eight years!" she went on. "It seems like yesterday. But I wouldn't have you think I'm occupying my old age in bitterness. If I have been misjudging Captain Ligny, it's only fair for me to make amends. So now, what are you going to do next, Mr. Carmichael?"

"I don't know," I said. "I haven't got a second *Walden* to lead me to another Miss Hancock."

"I should hope not," she said. "But I'm putting myself on your side of the fence for the time being. In your place, I would think about a very puzzling question. Why did your Mr. Ligny go to the boxing Friday night? After all his effort to make it look as though he had been drowned at Batemans Bay, he must go and see some pugilists five hundred miles away. Have you thought of that, Mr. Carmichael?"

I told myself that Miss Hancock's mind was as bright as her eyes.

"I have puzzled over that," I said. "So far, no answer has come up."

"He disappeared from the stadium when he learned he had been recognized," persisted Miss Hancock. "For him, that must have been a startling moment."

"I think that must be accepted."

"Why did *you* go to the boxing, Mr. Carmichael?"

"Not to meet Ligny," I said. "No, I went there because—" A lightning thought exploded in my mind like a flash revealing miles of black countryside. I hoped that Miss Hancock would overlook my hesitation. She didn't want to share her sins, and I didn't want to share my inspirations. "I went there to see the fighting," I said. "There was a good bill that night."

"I can only conclude your Mr. Ligny went to the stadium to meet somebody," Miss Hancock said. "Which doesn't help us at all, either on one side of the fence or on the other. But it's possible a more thorough discussion will bear fruit, and so I have a suggestion, Mr. Carmichael."

She eyed me as though checking an estimate that needed verifying. I did not speak.

"It's rather late in the afternoon for sight-seeing," she said. "But I do want you to see the places where Elspeth and I watched Captain Ligny and his men in action—the northwest scarp on the Mount and poor old Uncle Mick Hancock's hut. I often go to the crater—it's a favorite haunt of mine—but I've never been back to the hut since that dreadful fight. You can understand why, I think, but looking at these places could give us another lead to Mr. Ligny. So Mr. Carmichael, I suggest you stay here tonight and tomorrow I'll show you round."

I comprehended that Miss Hancock was telling me, as she had promised, what she thought of me.

5

Pleading urgent business in Melbourne, I did not stay despite the tempting prospect of exploring Mount Worriong and Mick's Hollow with Miss Hancock. The urgent business was very real, though I had been careful not to let Miss Hancock suspect it had had no existence until she asked me why I had gone to the stadium.

I had gone there because I was interested in one of the fighters. Ligny also could have been interested in one of the fighters. That was the inspiration. Though none of the names of the boxers at Festival Hall held meaning for me, not in the way the names of Ligny and Martin had in Miss Hancock's diary, I had remembered that many pugilists fought under assumed names. The lad who had worked for me, Leslie Holmes, was known in the ring as Billy Aden; in his case, when he had started fighting he didn't want his mother to know. It could be, then, there were other *noms de guerre* on Friday night's bill.

A long shot, but one that could not be ignored. There was a man called John Morgan in Melbourne whom I had known since we were schoolboys. A journalist, Morgan had by virtue of his prowess with bat and ball and boxing gloves blossomed out into an astute sportswriter on a city morning daily. He would have the information I sought.

As soon as I arrived back at my motel, I telephoned Morgan's office and luckily found him in. After the normal felicitations, I broached my inquiry—the actual names of the fighters at Festival Hall last Friday night. That was, of course, if they did fight under pseudonyms.

I parried Morgan's curiosity, and after he had consulted his files, he told me that out of the eight fighters on Friday night's bill, two used pseudonyms—Billy Aden, welterweight, real name Leslie Holmes (which of course I already knew), and Red Aherne, the heavyweight champion, who had defended his title successfully—real name Malcolm Blair.

Blair! Ligny, Martin, Giles and Blair! The long shot had come off. I had no proof, not a skerrick of evidence, but I felt I could act on the assumption that Ligny had gone to Festival Hall because Malcolm Blair was fighting.

"Tell me, John," I said, "what do you know about Malcolm Blair?"

"As a fighter or a man or what?"

"A potted biography."

"A queer request from you!" said Morgan. "All right. Malcolm Blair is thirty years old and married, though no progeny so far. In private life he is a cattle breeder at Mahon's Crossing in East Gippsland. His professional address is James Lloyd's gymnasium in North Melbourne, though you wouldn't find him there now; with the fight over, he would be back at Mahon's Crossing. He's been the heavyweight champ for five years, but his reign mightn't last much longer. It's no secret his only interest in fighting was to get himself a good farm, and I hear he's paid off the Mahon's Crossing place, so I wouldn't be surprised if he relinquishes the title. As I said, he's thirty now."

"What about his parents, John?"

"Both dead. He's a Legacy boy. His father was killed in the Second War."

I understood the significance of "Legacy boy." I was a member of Legacy, the Australian association of ex-servicemen whose sole object was the welfare of dead servicemen's children.

"Was his father's name Garrett Blair?" I asked.

"Just a moment, Sandy . . . Yes, that's right. Garrett Blair was his father."

I recalled the big fighter I had seen at Festival Hall, a beautiful figure of a man with short coppery hair, gray eyes and granite chin. I speculated whether Miss Hancock, had she been at the fight, could have recognized Garrett Blair in his son.

"One thing more, John. What kind of man is Malcolm Blair—approachable?"

"Not in the ring, Sandy. Incidentally, he's never called Red Aherne except when fighting. But if I take your inquiry correctly, he's a pleasant, courteous fellow, for Legacy have made a good job of him. An ornament to the profession, as we say in the papers—as long as your business with him is legitimate. Is it?"

I could feel Morgan's curiosity scorching the line.

"Listen, John," I said. "I'm grateful for your help. I wish I could tell you all about it, but I can only say thanks very much."

Which, I'm afraid, was highly unsatisfactory for Morgan. . . .

Early next morning, Tuesday, August 19, I was on Princess Highway, traveling fast. I was also traveling hopefully. Twenty miles north from the highway, Mahon's Crossing lay in a Gippsland glen against the mistily blue backdrop of the alps. The valley was green and gold with early spring, but I saw no Walden Pond contour, no feature, no trait, that was reminiscent of Ligny's lake. That had been too much to hope for.

A small school, a tiny church and a country store stood among gums and poplars and wattles on the bank of a sluggish creek. After getting directions from the store, I drove over a bridge and continued up the valley until I came to a white-painted gate on the right-hand side of the road. On one of the gateposts was a mailbox labeled "Blair."

It seemed that Malcolm Blair the cattle breeder was just as efficient as Red Aherne the heavyweight champion. Well-grassed paddocks, trim fences, clumps of white gums, fat Herefords, ornamental trees lining a graveled drive, neat outbuildings, hay sheds, stockyards, the pale green roof of a house partly hidden behind shorn hedges.

The man who possessed such a kingdom would never tolerate a stranger prying into his affairs, and I foresaw myself being turfed out of this place. Well, no matter. I drove along the drive. Near the hedge, the drive divided, one prong going on to the outbuildings, the other leading into the house grounds. Two men busy in the stockyards glanced at me, then went on with their work. Neither of them was Malcolm Blair. I turned into the garden and halted before the front veranda.

A radio was dispensing a pop melody somewhere in the house, and mingling with the music were two female voices conversing animatedly. When I mounted the steps and pressed the bell button, the conversation broke off abruptly, and two young fair-haired women, evidently sisters, appeared and examined me through a screen door. One wore a wedding ring, and so I made a guess.

"Mrs. Blair?"

"Yes."

"My name is Carmichael, Mrs. Blair, Sandy Carmichael. Could I see Mr. Blair, please?"

"Malcolm?" she said. "He's not in at the moment."

"I'm sorry," I said, deducing her husband *was* in and she wanted to get rid of a stranger who could be a peddler or something just as obnoxious. But I was mistaken. Mrs. Blair opened the screen door, stepped out on the veranda and gazed over the hedge toward the road.

"He'll be here in two or three minutes," she said. "He's been out on his morning run," she added, as if the explanation wasn't really necessary.

Looking in the direction she indicated, I saw a man clad in khaki shorts racing down the side of a hill beyond the road, and I thought of Miss Hancock's description of the four men hurtling down Mount Worriong.

"Would you like to sit here?" said Mrs. Blair. "Or would you prefer to come inside?"

"The veranda, thank you. I don't want to be in your way."

"I'll tell Malcolm you're here as soon as he gets in," Mrs. Blair said, and she and her sister retreated.

I sat down on a settee, and the running figure sank below the level of the hedge. The only sound was the radio until I caught a glimpse of Malcolm Blair through the hedge, sprinting the final stretch. Then uproar broke out. Several dogs at the rear of the establishment started barking, apparently in welcome. He ran around to the back of the house and the hullabaloo of his arrival subsided. A woman's voice spoke. There were quick footsteps in the passage, and a sweating face peered through the screen door.

"Good morning," Malcolm Blair said. His speech was free of slurred consonants and tortured vowels. "Just give me a chance for a shower and I'll be with you."

He retired. I waited seven minutes, and then he came out onto the veranda, clad in brown pullover, khaki slacks and moccasins. His coppery hair was smooth and damp, and his face showed the bruises he had taken in Friday night's battering at Festival Hall. I am not small, but his size and coiled strength and fighter's jaw and unwinking gray eyes made me feel insignificant. He didn't smile, and he didn't offer to shake hands.

"Now, Mr. Carmichael, what do you want?"

"Mr. Blair," I said, plunging straight into the heart of the matter, "I'm looking for a man named Lewis Ligny. By what I have heard, you might be able to help me to find him."

Though he did not move, I had a vivid impression of his gathering himself up for an explosion of violent action.

"Who are you?" he said. "A policeman?"

"No. Just a friend of Lewis Ligny."

"A friend?" There was danger in his eyes. Abruptly he said, "Sit down, Mr. Carmichael."

We seated ourselves side by side on the settee and I gauged I was safe for the time being.

"You're the second man to come here asking about Lewis Ligny," he said. "The first man was here two days ago— Sunday."

"A policeman, Mr. Blair?"

"No."

"Could I ask for his name?"

"No names, no pack drill, Mr. Carmichael." Leaning back, Blair crossed his legs, and I watched the slow powerful pulse in the dangling foot. "You say you are looking for Lewis Ligny. The first man didn't say if he was looking for Ligny. He only wanted to know what I knew about him. But you claim you are looking for him and, as well, you are a friend of his."

"That is right."

"Very well," said Blair. He turned his head toward the door. "Judith!"

"Yes, Mal."

"Would you mind bringing out Saturday's paper, please?"

Mrs. Blair duly appeared with a newspaper, one that had, on the back page, the story of Red Aherne's championship fight at Festival Hall. But Blair ignored this. When his wife was gone, he opened the paper at an unobtrusive item that told of Lewis Ligny's disappearance from the rocks at Batemans Bay and the presumption of his death by drowning.

"The other fellow on Sunday drew my notice to this item," Blair said, "but no more than that. He made no suggestion

61

the story wasn't true. But you are asking me to help find Ligny. What's that mean?"

"It means he did not drown," I said.

"How do you know that?"

"I saw him after he was supposed to have disappeared at Batemans Bay."

"I'd like to hear the explanation," he said.

Thereupon, as I had done with Miss Hancock though much more briefly, I related what I knew of Ligny and what I thought of him. I did not mention my purloining Thoreau's *Walden,* but I spoke, without revealing Miss Hancock's identity, of her diary and the names Ligny, Martin, Giles and Blair, and I went on to describe my seeing Ligny at Festival Hall on Friday night, which made Blair glower with fresh suspicion.

"Then late yesterday evening," I said, "I discovered that Red Aherne was really Malcolm Blair, the son of Garrett Blair, killed in the Second War. And that's why I am here, talking to you."

"Who told you Garrett Blair was my father?"

"No names, no pack drill," I said.

Blair pulled a face at that.

"You claim you're a friend of Ligny?" he said.

"Yes—as far as I'm able to be."

"The other man on Sunday asked me if I'd ever met Ligny," Blair said. "I told him never. I told him also I hadn't known before he came on Sunday if Ligny was alive or dead, but if ever I meet Ligny, I would not call him a friend. He killed my father."

I sat rigid. Blair was just as still. The radio inside the house had the field to itself.

"You must have solid reason to make such an extraordinary claim," I said at last.

"I have," Blair said somberly. "And to be fair with you, I'll show you what I showed to the other man. Excuse me."

He fetched a small table from the end of the veranda and

placed it in front of me. Then he went inside to return quickly with several rubber-banded bundles of letters. He put the letters on the table, removed the rubber bands, sat down beside me and let his cold gray eyes rove over the paddocks. The early morning mists had dissolved, the sun had moved over, the trees on the hills had taken a darker tint, and the alps in the background were deep blue.

"Not a bad place, Mahon's Crossing," Blair said, looking at his fat Herefords. "It's a good place, and I own a fair share of it. As long as I can remember, I wanted to be a cattleman, and fighting was the way to get it. I suppose I'm lucky in having the strength"—he stretched out his right arm and clenched the fist—"to be a first-class fighter. But as for this farm and the house and the cattle and my wife—well, in one way, I have to thank your friend Ligny for all of them. Smoke, if you like."

He watched as I filled my pipe and put a match to it.

"I like a pipe," he said. "I'll get back to it when I give up fighting. . . . I'm a Legacy boy and I'm a Legacy boy because my father was killed in the war—'killed accidentally on active service,' as they call it. My mother died while I was still young, and Legacy looked after me ever since. Family, schooling, guidance when I started fighting, money when I needed it—there were times when I was up against it and the money would come—I owe all that to Legacy. In a couple of weeks' time, in the school vacation, you'll see a mob of Legacy kids here having a holiday. It's one way I can show my thanks to Legacy. There are other ways too, but let that go. I'm here because my father was killed in the war.

"I never knew him. I was about six months old when he sailed for the Middle East in 1940, and I was about twenty-one months when he came back to Australia in 1941. So the only thing I know of him, apart from hearsay, is these letters. He wrote them to my mother in 1940 and 1941.

"I was born in Melbourne, Mr. Carmichael. My mother was living with her parents, and after I came on the scene, she started working in a munitions factory. I don't think she liked it, but she was able to take a holiday in 1941 when my father arrived back from the Middle East: he had a leave of twenty-one days. I'm telling you this to explain the letters—rather, the parts I read out to you. You won't want to hear everything my father wrote, only the parts dealing with—well—your friend."

That was fair enough. I didn't wish to hear what a soldier had to say to his wife—not the things that had concerned themselves only. Blair sifted through the letters, and I saw that the envelopes had been numbered consecutively. He picked up the one numbered 54, drew out the contents and flattened the sheets on his knee. It was evident that Sergeant Garrett Blair had been a voluminous correspondent.

"According to my mother," said Blair, "this letter was written in the Western Desert. It is dated 20/2/41, and this is what he said—that is, the part you'd be interested in.

"Today I've had an exciting surprise. I guess it will please you when I'm able to tell you what it is. It's a move for me and I'm looking forward to it. The fly in the ointment is saying good-bye to all the fellows in this unit. They're wonderful blokes. If the new crowd is half as good, I'll be lucky. . . ."

Blair returned the letter to its envelope. "The surprise," he said, "was the news he was being returned to Australia to take up a special course. And of course my mother found out what the surprise was when he landed suddenly home on twenty-one days' leave. He didn't know what the course was. At least, he said he didn't. My guess is he did know but wasn't allowed to tell. Anyway, he was rather thrilled about it because it looked as though he would come out of it with a commission. Lieutenant Garrett Blair would look better than Sergeant Garrett Blair."

I wondered whether in looking at his son I was getting a slant into the mind of Sergeant Blair. Maybe. Blair opened the envelope marked 59.

"Dated 18/6/41," he said. "Written from Puckapunyal, so my mother said, and she wrote Puckapunyal on it, though I don't know how she found out. Well, here it is, and you'll see his rosy optimism died fast:

"I duly reported in Royal Park at 0800 hours and I was as cold and miserable as the weather. I don't know why every time I have to return from leave coincides with foul weather. But that does not wipe out the preceding twenty-one days. It was a wonderful leave, Alison.

"I eventually discovered the orderly office I had to report to, and there I met my new companions. There were only four of us! Captain ―― ――, W.O. ―― ――, Sgt. ―― ―― and me. . . ."

Breaking off from his reading, Blair said, "The names were heavily blacked out. See for yourself."

He held the sheet up with the writing turned away from me, but the black bars he spoke of were visible through the paper.

"Captain Ligny, W.O. Martin and Sergeant Giles, of course," Blair said. He resumed reading.

"We put our kits into a ute and piled in ourselves, the ―― and the ―― in the front and ―― and me in the back, and it was a good thing the ute was covered. The rain poured down, but in spite of that we arrived safely at our destination, though rather like Hamlet's traveler. . . ."

Blair said, "My father was something of a literary man, but my mother was no scholar and it took her some time to work out what he meant by Hamlet's traveler. He couldn't explain it himself because she never saw him after that last leave, but in the end she fathomed the reference for herself."

Blair produced a piece of paper from the same envelope and handed it to me. On it an unskilled hand had written:

> Who would fardels bear,
> To grunt and sweat under a weary life,
> But that the dread of something after death,―

The undiscovered country, from whose bourn
No traveler returns,—puzzles the will.

Hamlet, Act III, Sc. 1

"He already knew his future was black," Blair said. "Yes—
'to grunt and sweat under a weary life.' He already knew Captain Ligny was no friend of his."

He put the letter and the excerpt from Hamlet back into
the envelope and took up letter number 64.

"This is an important one," he said. "It's dated 22/8/41,
and it was sneaked out by a soldier going on leave, and he
personally delivered it to my mother at home. This is how it
goes:

"Here we are at Bonegilla. We got here two days ago and I was
lucky enough to find an old mate who will give you this letter himself. I won't name him in case—a remote possibility, of course—
somebody official lights on this.

"It gives me a chance to tell you something of what's happening
to us. I can't, you understand, tell you what we're engaged on. It's
pretty big, Alison, and frightening, and if word gets out about it,
I'm going to make sure they can't blame me. Or, more importantly,
you!

"It's very hard work, physically and mentally. We go from dawn
till far after dark; sometimes we get no more than three or four
hours of sleep a day. But I wouldn't mind the risk or hard work or
the long study if only Captain Ligny was fair and decent.

"Apparently we have been picked by our special attributes. We
are all big, strong, athletic. We are—or are supposed to be—very
bright birds intellectually. We are said to be superbly balanced psy-
chologically. If that means we are able to take punishment without
whimpering, maybe the experts are right with three of us.

"Hugh Martin is quiet, tough, hard-working, frank and open.
There are no secrets with Hugh. He is not married and he talks a
good deal about his family in Kalgoorlie—father, mother and
young brother. As you can guess, Hugh was a miner in Civvy Street.

"Wilfrid Giles is a different kettle of fish. He's just as hard and
strong as Hugh and game as they come. He's a garrulous chap,
always jesting in an acid style; yet with all his talk he doesn't give
anything away about himself. I do not know yet what he was in

prewar days, or if he has a family, though he once told me he had nobody in the world to care a damn about him—which is not the same thing as saying he has no family. A lone wolf, he calls himself. An unhappy lone wolf, I'd judge. In spite of this, I like him immensely.

"In the few weeks we've been together, Hugh, Wilfrid and I have become close friends. But Captain Ligny is an utter bastard. Hugh was brought down from Darwin to start on this project. Wilfrid came down from Rabaul and of course I was hauled back from the Western Desert. Where Captain Ligny came from, I don't know, but if he would have been in New Britain or Malaya or the Western Desert, his own men would have shot him long ago.

"He is savage with us all, but particularly with Wilfrid Giles. Somehow I feel Captain Ligny and Wilfrid have met before we all reported in at Royal Park, and because of this previous encounter, Hugh Martin and I are suffering, too. I don't like the signs. . . ."

"Well, what do you think of your friend now?" Blair said. "The badge in your lapel means you've been in the army. What would you have done with Captain Ligny?"

"I withhold judgment," I said unhappily. "Anything more?"

"Oh, my word, Mr. Carmichael."

He reached for another letter. The envelope bore the number 75.

"Just as important as the last one," he said. "It's dated 14/9/41."

I straightened up, for this date fell into the compass of Miss Hancock's diary.

Blair began to read:

"This is being written in the middle of Saturday night—rather, in the early hours of Sunday morning. Hugh is also writing a letter home and Wilfrid is keeping nit. Wilfrid has discovered a way of smuggling letters out and as long as the bastard (you know who) doesn't wake up to the lurk, you'll get others in the same way.

"We arrived at Mount Worriong last Monday and we've got regal quarters, the homestead of an old family called Hancock, impressed by the army. Up to our arrival, it has been used as a recuperation center for sick personnel. With our coming it has been turned into the headquarters of Plan Jumbuk. Plan Jumbuk is the very secret project we're engaged on, but what it is we don't know —at least Hugh, Wilfrid and I don't, except it has something in part to do with explosives.

"There is an old extinct volcano not far from the homestead. We gallop up and down the volcano several times a day, and in between, we have unarmed combat and mysterious mental exercises such as map reading while blindfolded. Captain Ligny has condescended to tell us we're being conditioned much like Pavlov's dogs to react quickly, surely, automatically, to alarming situations without thinking or feeling.

"For the last, he's doing his damnedest to grind any emotion out of us. Yet there seems to be another side to him, or maybe he's playing on us in a subtle way. When the army turfed the Hancocks out of their homestead (I guess they got compensation), they retired to a house perched on the side of the extinct volcano. It's called Worriong Cottage. Whatever his motives, Captain Ligny took us to Worriong Cottage to meet the Hancocks. There are four of them— Mr. Quentin Hancock, his wife Royena, their daugher Elspeth, and Miss Rhoda Hancock, Mr. Hancock's stately sister. There is another member of the family, Wesley, a son, somewhere in the army, so we couldn't see *him*.

"The daughter Elspeth is a pretty girl and she fell straightaway for Wilfrid, and apparently Wilfrid responded, and right under Captain Ligny's nose, though Wilfrid has emphatically denied any romantic attachment. In fact, he is profanely upset about it, but it's a lovely turn-up for Hugh and me. Elspeth has undertaken to get any letters we write out to the post office, and this dead-of-night writing is the result. We have a free hour or two this afternoon and we'll accidentally call on the Hancocks and slip our letters to Elspeth.

"If Captain Ligny wasn't such a bloody pig, I would suggest your coming up to Mount Worriong one weekend. There's a decent pub in the township some miles away. But of course it's not possible with Ligny. . . ."

Well, I thought, it looked as though the gaps in Miss Hancock's diary would continue to be gaps. But that wasn't important. What was important was the mounting foreboding that my faith in Ligny would take a supreme buffeting.

"So it was one of the Hancocks you saw yesterday," Blair said. "I would bet it was Elspeth."

"No," I said, not bothering to quibble. "It was her aunt Rhoda. All the other Hancocks have been dead for years."

"She must be old."

"Eighty-one."

Blair dismissed Miss Hancock with a shake of his head.

"Only one letter to go," he said. He abstracted a single sheet from an envelope. "Just a short note, dated 7/10/41 . . .

"All hell today, Alison. Captain Ligny nearly killed Wilfrid this morning in unarmed combat. Both did their block* and spat words at each other, confirming my impression they knew each other long before we started this course. The fight became serious, and Hugh Martin and I were on the point of intervening when Miss Hancock and Elspeth came on the scene. So we're being hoisted out—to where, I've no idea, but wherever it is, Captain Ligny has no happy fate in store for us. Wilfrid says that if we drop our letters out the back of the ute near the main gate, Elspeth will be there to pick them up. . . ."

Blair replaced the note in its envelope and methodically assembled the letters into their various bundles. He said, "There are more, as you see, but all routine. The sort of thing that reads, 'I'm very well, and I hope you and the kid are well, too,' all countersigned by Captain Ligny. In the end, my mother received official word my father had been killed accidentally. Accidentally! Accidentally killed by your friend."

"That's only an opinion."

"It is. But it's right." Blair leaned back in the settee and his jaw hardened. "I've made inquiries. I've asked the military people what happened and they said the accident happened in an explosion. But in the way of this world, Mr. Carmichael, a champion boxer is an important figure, and an army officer whispered to me the killing of my father and the

* Lost their tempers.

69

other two men was classified, which means never to be made public in any circumstances whatever. Now have you made your judgment?"

"We haven't got all the facts yet," I said.

"You're dying hard," Blair said. "All right. Here's another thing. You said your seeing Ligny at Festival Hall started you on his trail. But have you any idea why he was there?"

"Ideas are not facts," I said lamely.

"Well, I know why he was there," Blair said. "We know Ligny worked in the army with three men—Martin, Giles, Blair. It was easy to discover I was Malcolm Blair, the son of Garrett Blair. Easy for you. Much easier for Ligny, for he knew Garrett Blair had a son called Malcolm: he censored my father's letters. I wonder how many of my fights he watched just to see me."

"For heaven's sake, why?"

"Just to gloat over the son of the man he killed."

"Good God! How you must hate him!"

"Wouldn't you?"

After that, there was not much that could be said, but I did try for more information. I asked Blair if he had ever attempted to get in touch with the relatives of Martin or Giles. He had never thought of that, he said, though he knew where Martin's family could be located. But it was conviction that Giles had no relatives, and the same went for Ligny; both had been lone wolves, in Garrett Blair's phrase.

Then I took out my pocketbook and, on a clean page, drew the outline of Ligny's lake, and it must have been a fair copy for Blair immediately detected the likeness to a one-legged ewe.

"Does it make you think of anything?" I asked. "That is, besides a crippled Merino?"

Shaking his head, he said no, and in the pause that followed came the voice of Mrs. Blair speaking through the screen door.

"I'm sorry, Mr. Carmichael, but the police are looking for you."

70

6

I learned then what my journalist friend Morgan had meant by saying Malcolm Blair was a pleasant, courteous fellow as long as your business with him was legitimate. For a long minute I stood in peril of his mighty fists. His wife's explanation that she had just heard a radio message that the police wished to locate a Mr. Alexander Carmichael, thought to be traveling somewhere in Victoria in a black Falcon V8, did not placate him. Keeping me at his side, he insisted himself on ringing the Bairnsdale police, and I had to listen while he conversed, none too politely, with the officer he raised.

He turned to me suddenly.

"Do you own a caravan?"

"Yes."

"Where is it now?"

"Marchmont Caravan Park, Seymour."

"What is its number?"

"GYM 2021."

After relaying this information to the officer in Bairnsdale, he handed the receiver over to me so that I could get at first hand the news that thieves or vandals had burgled my caravan and the interior was now a mess.

"A bad business," Blair said when I had hung up and explained that my caravan was my headquarters, office and home. "Did you keep any money there?" he asked, his hostility dissipated.

"Yes, a sum held in reserve. But it's cunningly hidden, and the thieves might have missed it."

"Hope so," said Blair. "It could have been worse though. They could have taken caravan and all."

"Not likely under Len Marchmont's eye," I said.

"I expect you're starting back straightaway," said Blair.

"Yes." I looked over the shining valley and the hills and the cattle. No wonder Blair had fought for a stake in Mahon's Crossing. I said, "Thanks for what you've done. If I have to come for further help, may I?"

"Anytime you like. But remember, your friend is not my friend."

For a second or two I thought of asking him for the name of the man who had preceded me in inquiries in the events of twenty-eight years ago. But I prudently decided not to press my luck too far, and I took my leave of Mrs. Blair and her sister (whose name I did not learn), shook hands with Blair and started off for Seymour.

Mahon's Crossing is about two hundred miles east of Melbourne, and the city is sixty miles south of Seymour, and there is no practicable shortcut. Nevertheless, I made good time, pausing only for petrol and a quick lunch, and it was just on seven-thirty when I crossed the new bridge over the Goulburn River at Seymour. A young moon glimmered on the water, and the granite hills were dark and cold, and mist was shrouding the ancient red gums.

A few minutes later, I pulled up on the concrete drive in front of Len Marchmont's combined office and living quarters. I saw a light shining through the office window. I got out of the car, walked past Len's establishment and glanced over the lines of caravans and parked cars huddled under sheltering gums. I saw my caravan in its usual position a few yards from the Marchmonts' end wall. Len and Beth and I were old friends, and whenever I wanted to leave the caravan with them, they invariably sited it where they could watch over it while I was away.

Somebody had managed to get under their guard this time. But I couldn't poke into the caravan without letting them know I had arrived. Retracing my steps, I knocked on the office door, and Len Marchmont emerged to greet me. A short, broad man, he eyed me with nothing of his habitual cheerfulness.

"We were expecting you," he said. "The police told us they'd found you in East Gippsland. I'm sorry, Sandy."

"It could have happened to anyone," I said.

"But we're responsible, Sandy. We were in charge of it. I'd hate this to happen to anyone, but especially to you."

"Don't let it worry you," I said. "But I suppose we'd better look at the damage."

"Not right away," Len said. "The police want to be on hand when you make an inventory, so they've sealed the caravan and I've got to ring them when you've arrived. You have time to come inside and say hullo to Beth and she'll get you something to eat. I'll bet you're hungry."

I went into the living quarters, shook hands with Beth, whose hazel eyes and chestnut hair always made me think of my sister Stella, and sat down to a meal of grilled steak and fried potatoes.

Detective Torbay of the Seymour C.I.B. came as I was drinking my second cup of coffee. He was a big fair man and he displayed the usual enigmatic air of detectives on duty. He and Len Marchmont and I proceeded to my caravan where the formality of breaking the seals occurred. The seals were strips of adhesive paper stuck at strategic positions on the door and the windows, and Detective Torbay had dated and initialed each of them. He went around the caravan, shining a torch onto the seals and making sure they were still intact. Satisfied they were as he had left them earlier, he tore them off, rolled them into little pellets and dropped them into his pocket.

"I'd have never noticed anything this morning except the door was open," Len said. "Whoever they were, they know how to open doors. None of your neighbors heard anything during the night."

"Cluey people," Torbay said. "Could I have your key, Mr. Carmichael?"

I gave him the key, and he inserted it into the keyhole. He turned the bolt back and forth several times.

"Yes, cluey," he said. "Nothing wrong with the lock."

He opened the door and the three of us went in and I switched on the lights. The police at Bairnsdale had described the interior as a mess. I would have called it a shambles only there wasn't any blood. I had built the caravan in three main compartments—kitchenette, sleeping berth and workroom or office. (I usually refer to the last-named as the fo'c'sle because it occupied the forward end over the tow bar.) As well, the caravan had the customary cupboards and cabinets and a small shower recess, not used, of course, when ablution sheds were available as in Len's park. Everything had been dragged out and strewn over chairs, tables and floors—tinned food-stuffs, cutlery, soap, tomato sauce, clothing, bedclothes, books, papers, instruments, pencils, typewriter. Even the refrigerator contents were scattered on the floor. Where the floor was visible, there were the marks of muddy boots, and everywhere on the ledges and shelves I saw the gray powder of fingerprint dust.

"Did you have anything valuable?" asked Torbay.

"They're all valuable to me."

"I mean," Torbay said patiently, "things thieves could sell quickly—watches, jewelry, electric shavers and so on."

"Well—some."

"We want you to find out if there's anything missing," said Torbay. "That's why we sealed the place up. No use searching without you on hand."

I could see that was good common sense. It was also obvious that the only way to answer Torbay's question was to get everything back into its rightful place. It seemed an appalling job, but both Len Marchmont and Torbay offered to help, and half an hour's work restored the caravan to something like its normal appearance.

There remained only one task. I went to the shelf over the refrigerator, took the ends of the front of the shelf and pulled out a shallow drawer. Putting the drawer on the table, I pointed at the banknotes held flat under small wire springs and said, "My hidden nest egg. It's safe."

"How much is there?" asked Torbay.

"Four hundred dollars."

"Count it, please."

I knew it was all there, but to satisfy Torbay I counted out twenty-five ten-dollar notes and thirty five-dollar notes.

"There you are," I said.

I tucked the notes under the wire springs and pushed the drawer back into the shelf. The detective examined the shelf, peered at each end and then pulled. The drawer stayed fast.

"You push in first, then twist right to left, then pull," I said, but I didn't offer a demonstration.

"Cluey," Torbay said. He deserted the drawer. "Well, anything missing?"

"I could find something is gone when I come to look specifically for it," I said, "but I would say at this moment—nothing."

"In that case, I would say vandals," Torbay said. "Only vandals usually not only clutter up your things but they also disfigure and destroy and befoul. Well, there doesn't appear anything we can do for the time. With your permission, I'll get back to the station."

"What about the footprints and the fingerprints?" I asked.

The detective stared, thinking at first I wanted him to clean the floor and tables and ledges. Then he caught my meaning. The foot marks were valueless, he said; they came from a common type of rubber boot. As for the prints, if it was necessary he would return on some future occasion to take my prints to compare with the others he had already garnered.

I comprehended that "some future occasion" really meant never. The police investigation into the outrage on my caravan was closed. I accompanied Detective Torbay and Len Marchmont outside. The air was raw, and the earlier mist had thickened into fog that made a blinding reflection for the glaring headlamps on the highway. I refused Len's invitation to drink coffee with Torbay and him (at mention of coffee, the detective thought the station could do without him for a little longer), and I watched the fog swallow them.

Thieves? Vandals? Only one person had broken into the caravan, not a mob, but I was too weary to go on from there. Lewis Ligny had shrunk into a small indistinct figure a long, long way from me. In bed, I lay listening to the water dropping from the red gums, and then I went to sleep.

The morning stirred to a fresh east wind, trundling fluffy clouds over the hills. The breeze had blown the fog away from the river and with it something of the fog in my brain. I took breakfast with the Marchmonts; then I returned to the caravan, got to work with vacuum cleaner and removed all traces of marauders and police.

It was time to review the situation, and I went to the fo'c'sle, sat down and lit a pipe. Last night I had been too tired to think, unable even to recall what Ligny looked like. Now my mind was in working order, and so two problems stood clearly before me.

First, the problem of Ligny's double image. The Ligny I knew and the Captain Ligny Miss Hancock and Malcolm Blair hated. One with the scarred face and appealing blue eyes; the other a tormentor of men. One the bookman, the garden lover; the other the would-be killer of Wilfrid Giles and who (according to Miss Hancock and Malcolm Blair) did kill him and Hugh Martin and Garrett Blair as well. One the creator of a model lake in the likeness of Walden Pond; the other a supreme bastard.

That was the great unconformity I had to reconcile.

Second, the problem of three men. I took a pencil and listed them.

1. The bludgeoner in my motel suite.
2. The man who had preceded me at Mahon's Crossing.
3. The vandal who had ransacked the caravan.

Almost at once, I perceived that this problem was but another facet of the double image, for I had already determined the attacker in the motel was Ligny. If Ligny was the attacker, then it was reasonable to assume it was also Ligny who had broken into the caravan. Obviously both forays had been made in search of something—for nothing had been stolen in each instance.

So far so good. The question of how Ligny located both my motel suite and the caravan raised an ugly head. I couldn't find an acceptable answer, and so, bypassing this stumbling block, I went on to consider the man who had beaten me to Mahon's Crossing. It was crystal clear that whether or no Ligny was concerned with the motel or the caravan, he was *not* Malcolm Blair's Sunday visitor. It was impossible to imagine Ligny asking Malcolm Blair for information about himself and drawing Blair's attention to the presumed drowning at Batemans Bay.

So the three men had been reduced to two. And then I thought, Two? Two was almost as illogical as three, and the question of how Ligny found my motel suite and caravan vanished. There was only one man camped on my trail, and his name was *not* Ligny.

This was satisfactory reasoning, though it did not identify the man dogging me or explain the purpose of the pursuit.

And then, unbidden, a possibility jolted my mind. As far as I was concerned, there was only one black mark against Ligny —his disappearance at Batemans Bay. But suppose, Carmichael, just suppose this man suspects I was also involved in the disappearance, that I was Ligny's accomplice in the faked drowning, and now he was trying to use me to point the way to Ligny?

The immediate result was a very ugly dilemma. Last Saturday, the day of my visit to Canberra, there had been three people (excluding Ligny and myself) who knew of my seeing Ligny at Festival Hall—my sister, Stella, her husband, Dan Hilary, and Edmund Martin.

The quandary persisted until late in the afternoon when I recalled a remark made by Miss Hancock when inviting me to stay at Worriong Cottage so that she could guide me to the crater and to Mick's Hollow. "I've never been back to the hut since that dreadful fight," she had said. If I took her up on that offer, she should have no objection.

I went to the office and asked Len Marchmont for his telephone directory, found the entry I needed and dialed Miss Hancock's number. Presently I heard a woman's voice say, "Worriong Cottage, the housekeeper speaking."

"Mrs. Riley? This is Sandy Carmichael, Mrs. Riley. Do you remember me?"

"Yes, Mr. Carmichael, I remember you very well. It's only two days since you were here. I guess you'd be wanting Miss Hancock?"

"Yes, please, Mrs. Riley."

"I'm sorry, Mr. Carmichael, but Miss Hancock is away. She's gone interstate."

Though I had no reason for it, I somehow felt Miss Hancock's sudden departure was a sequence of my visit to Worriong Cottage.

"How did she travel?" I asked curiously. "Air or train?"

"Goodness me! She went by car—her own car. Miss Hancock is a very experienced driver, Mr. Carmichael."

"I'm sure she is," I said, hastening to mollify the housekeeper. "When will she be back?"

"I really can't say. Perhaps a week, perhaps a fortnight. Miss Hancock wasn't sure herself."

"Well, when she returns, will you please tell her I called? Tell her, too, I'd like to repeat my visit to Worriong Cottage."

"I'll tell her, Mr. Carmichael."

I thanked Mrs. Riley and hung up. After all, Miss Hancock's presence wasn't necessary to my reconnaissance. She would have made it a little easier, that was all.

Early next morning I donned clothes suitable for bush work and set off for Mount Worriong, ninety miles west as the crow flies but considerably more by the shortest road route. The weather was kind, the roads winding through the hills were free of traffic, and I traveled fast. My watch showed half-past nine as I dropped down from the hills onto a graveled road and I saw the truncated cone of Mount Worriong six miles away. From this direction it was as aloof and solitary as when its lava had begun to cool. Only newly shorn sheep in the dew-wet paddocks and the hawks and magpies and crows witnessed my passing.

A mile from the cone, I slackened speed, looking for a junction which Miss Hancock's diary gave me reason to believe must exist. I found it at the foot of the mount, and from it a rough track wound away through the bush to the north. I paused a moment, decided the track would take a car and then went on. The road swung left over Mount Worriong's southern flank and here, now on bitumen, I arrived at a second junction. This offshoot was also bitumen, and it went steeply up to the gap where the old volcano had breached its cone and poured out its lava.

At the side of the road a sign fashioned in the shape of a pointing hand bore the behest, "Turn in for Mount Worriong Memorial Park." I followed the hand's direction.

Through the gap, the bitumen angled to the left and then went zigzagging up the crater's inner wall until it emerged onto the western scarp, where it ended in a parking sign.

I had the place to myself. I got out of the car, and carrying my binoculars, I went to a cairn surmounted by a bronze disc with arrows pointing to the salient features of the huge, wide-spreading landscape. Set in the cairn was a plaque bearing the names of Mount Worriong men who had served in the armed forces from the South African War to the Korean War. The addition of the Vietnam veterans was not yet effected, but I saw in the Second War contingent the name of Wesley Griffon Hancock. He was one Hancock I did not know anything of except that, like Uncle Mick Hancock, he had been something of an eccentric.

In the heel of the cairn was a tablet attesting that the Hon. James Smythe, M.L.C., President of the Worriong Shire, had on Sunday, 26 February, 1962, opened the Mount Worriong Memorial Park and its entry road.

So there had been no road when Miss Hancock climbed the mount to pick wattle blossoms and peep over the side to see Captain Ligny bullying his men up the slope and down again. I descried the roofs of Worriong Cottage away below me to the left. It must have been a climb, even for a Miss Hancock twenty-eight years younger. As for the men—I inclined right and gazed at the dizzy near-precipice of the northwest slope. No wonder one of them had fallen and plunged somersaulting until he lay still, and all he got for his pains had been Captain Ligny cursing him.

Twenty-eight years ago. All dead—Quentin, Royena, Elspeth, Martin, Giles, Blair—except for Miss Hancock and Captain Ligny. But the wattle was blooming again, the crater glowed with gold, and the sky arched to the faraway horizon.

I turned farther to the right, raised the binoculars to my eyes and started looking for Mick's Hollow. Miss Hancock had recorded that Uncle Mick Hancock's domain was two miles northeast from the mount. She had also written that, on

80

the day she and Elspeth discovered "the army in occupation" in the hollow, they had climbed down Chinese scrub.

The botanical name for Chinese scrub is *Cassinia arcuata*. This type of cassinia grows thickly in disturbed ground, usually old gold diggings, and where cassinia flourishes, so do ironbarks and boxtrees. Therefore, in this volcanic terrain of grassy paddocks and smooth-barked gums, the black trunks of ironbarks and boxes and the dull green cassinia and its fuzzy brown panicles should leap up in the binoculars.

The result turned out to be as I had thought.

With Mount Worriong looming over my left shoulder, I bumped and skidded along the track I had noticed previously. If I understood the diary rightly, this was the way Miss Hancock and Elspeth had trudged carrying binoculars, thermos flask and sandwiches, and their shoes must have gathered their quota of brown mud. The same brown mud spattered my car. Keeping my eyes closely on the track, I didn't realize I was nearing my destination until I saw that the brown mud had yielded to yellow clay just as slippery.

I stopped the car and got out. To the right, a ridge dropped gently to miles of rolling countryside stretching to the east and northeast. Behind was Mount Worriong lifting its flanks as though cut off in unfulfilled oblation. In front, to the northwest, were yellow gravel and hungry grass and ironbarks and boxes and the thick Chinese scrub. Beyond the trees and scrub, nothing; there the ground dipped into Mick's Hollow.

I made for the cassinia and it enveloped me, and its strong aromatic odor tickled my nose. The ground pitched swiftly, and I clambered down carefully, hanging onto rocky outcrops and the butts of the scrub. I descended two hundred feet or more; then the grade eased, the scrub opened up, and I could see into Mick's Hollow.

Uncle Mick Hancock must have been not only a hermit but a hater of himself as well, else he wouldn't have cloistered himself in such a desolate spot. Ugly rocks, sparse grass struggling through sand (perhaps remnants of the creek sand Captain Ligny and his men had carted in), a slab-built hut now on the verge of collapse, a chimney of unshaped sandstone, a corrugated iron water tank rusted through. No flowers or the semblance of a garden, and all hemmed in by the monotonous cassinia.

The door was partly open, hanging from broken hinges. I walked quietly across the clearing, pushed past the sagging door and went in. And then I stopped, unable to move. There was a woman in this dim, dingy, forsaken hut. She could have been the wraith of one of the long-dead Hancock women. But she was no wraith. She was my sister, Stella, and she had in her hands the black rectangle of board I had hoped to find.

7

After exploding into terse ejaculations, Stella and I stared at each other, marooned in a silence that crackled with consternation and unspoken challenge and, on my part, anger.

Steady, Sandy, I thought, desperately; you could bring all hell about you, and Stella, too. Throttling my wrath into submission, I took my sister by the elbow and led her outside to an outcropping bench of sandstone.

We sat down uneasily side by side. Not yet ready to speak, I lifted the board from Stella's hands. It was a plasticine modeling board, and on it was the model that had been kneaded twenty-eight years ago, a one-legged sheep with exaggerated ribs—a starving sheep just as Miss Hancock's diary had described it. The plasticine had solidified, and it stuck to the board like concrete. Dust lay thickly over it, and the dust transferred itself to my hands. Stella was rubbing the grime from her fingers with a handkerchief.

"Well," I said, striving for a normal tone, "this is a surprise. If only I'd known, we could have come here together. It would have saved us both from a devil of a jolt."

Stella wore an outfit I had often seen—brown slacks and a fawn woolen pullover, which she used for hiking in the bush. She put the handkerchief into the pocket of her slacks, and from the pocket of the pullover she took a cigarette case. I lit a match for her.

"Thanks," she said.

"Well?" I asked.

Her glance was long and thoughtful.

"Yes," she said. "You're boiling with questions, but I'm afraid I have nothing to say. Except I'm very glad it was you who walked in just now"—she patted my hand—"but for anything else, I'm sorry, brother."

"I can't quite accept that as good enough in the circumstances," I said with careful attention to both words and manner. "Finding my sister in this godforsaken hole four hundred miles from home and husband deserves some little explanation."

"Sorry," she said, surprising me with the luminous commiseration in her hazel eyes. "Thinking it out for yourself would be better for both of us. I don't want any quarreling, Sandy."

I remembered that (as I had so painfully realized yesterday) on Saturday there had been three people, leaving out Ligny and myself, who knew I had seen Ligny at Festival Hall—Stella, her husband, Dan, and Edmund Martin. But why should she have to feel sorry for me?

"Is Dan here, too?" I said.

"Dan? Goodness, no."

"Does he know you are here?"

"I'm not in the habit of going anywhere without telling Dan," Stella said mildly.

"Then is Edmund Martin here?"

"He is *not,*" Stella said. "What do you think of me?"

That was something, anyway.

"When did you leave Canberra?" I asked.

"Two o'clock this morning."

"Not bad going. Where's your car now?"

She pointed in a westerly direction.

"Over there, about a quarter of a mile away. There's a gravel road running five miles in from the Midland Highway," she said.

But that was all I could get from my sister. She neither affirmed nor denied that Dan had planned the trip or Edmund Martin had any part in it, or she had substituted for either of them, or the target of the journey was the plasticine model, or she knew she was in a place called Mick's Hollow, or she had ever heard of a family called Hancock.

"Well," I said with heavy sarcasm, "have you ever heard tell of a man called Lewis Ligny?"

Stella maintained her detached air of pity. Looking around in exasperation, I became mindful again of the board in my hands, and at this, the idea occurred that though I had found Stella clutching the board, it might have been only part of the purpose of her journey.

Placing the board beside Stella, I returned to the hut and contemplated the uninviting interior. The rickety table, the broken chair, the ramshackle cupboard. The wooden bunk and filthy blankets. The ancient ashes in the fireplace. The rusty pots, pans, tins, bottles and stoved-in boxes. The heaps of rubbish and leaves and papers and magazines that rats had nested in. The dust and cobwebs. And the now-splintered blackboard Captain Ligny had used in his blindfold instruction.

I launched into the job of rummaging through this filthy debris. Twenty minutes later and badly in need of a bath, I surveyed the fruits of my search:

1. A modeling board that had meaningless traces of the plasticine it had carried. I threw it away.
2. A dirty crumpled sheet of quarto paper, used on both sides.
3. A stained and tattered birthday card.

The last-named bore a handwritten inscription:

To Uncle Mick
From your loving grandnephew,
Wesley.
From one misfit to another.

I thought this card could be regarded as a verification of Miss Hancock's statement that Wesley, like Uncle Mick, had not marched in step with the main body of Hancocks. It aroused a wonder at the number and virulence of family rows it implied. No doubt Miss Hancock's "other" diary would have the details. Though the card had nothing to do with Ligny, I deposited it in my wallet and turned to taking stock of the various significances of the second find.

On one side, the quarto sheet bore a rough delineation in pencil of the familiar Merino shape, and under it were written the words: *The bastard is at his dirty work again.* Through the words was a strong black line as though someone looking over the writer's shoulder had angrily crossed the comment out.

On the reverse was a peculiar graph in which the vertical axis rose up the right-hand border, and the horizontal axis extended to the left. The vertical scale mounted in geometrical progression of 2 to 1,048,576, but the horizontal scale, instead of starting from the right, started on the left and traveled to the right in powers of 10 to finish with 10,000,000 coinciding with the 0 of the vertical scale.

The curve plotted on the graph began at the 0 of the horizontal scale and curled up gently to the right until about halfway. There a dotted line continued the curve in a swift rise that terminated near the top of the vertical scale. On the curve were annotations printed in a small hand, all but two of them on the continuous line. At the foot of the curve was the word *Grenade.* Then followed in quick succession *Gunpowder, Dynamite, Gelignite, Land Mine, Shrapnel, H.E. Shell, Bomb 250, Bomb 1000* and *Blockbuster.* Culminating at the top of the dotted section (the dots apparently indicating a hypothetical extension of the curve) was *Krakatoa.* I wondered why A-Bomb and H-Bomb had been omitted, and then I remembered that in 1941 atomic and nuclear bombs had not yet dawned on an unsuspecting world.

There were two annotations that at first glance seemed to have no bearing on explosions or explosives, and I guessed there had been nobody peering over the writer's shoulder as he made them. One was the ringed word *Me* adjacent to the word *Grenade;* the other was the name *Ligny,* also encircled, just under *Krakatoa.*

I recalled that in one of his letters Sergeant Garrett Blair had told his wife he and the men with him were engaged in a secret project designated Plan Jumbuk that had partly to do with explosions. And this graph would appear to refer to the comparative strengths of explosives, though whether in demolitionary power or in lethal range was obscure.

But why the ringed *Me* and *Ligny?* A grim joke, perhaps, *Me* being sited in the bottom killing range and *Ligny* being ranked with Krakatoa. On the other hand, it might have implied that *Me* could be killed easily, while *Ligny* was like the late Rasputin: he would require a lot of butchering. At least, whether the annotations were a joke or not, they added to the impression of steaming tension between Captain Ligny and his men.

My mind harked back to Plan Jumbuk. *Jumbuk* was one of the aboriginal names for sheep. *Jumbuk* was also the name of a little district in South Gippsland. There in Jumbuk, I shouted silently to myself, I could find Ligny. Then I reminded myself I was acquainted with Jumbuk the settlement and there was nothing in its hills and valleys that looked like a one-legged Merino ewe, no configuration that resembled Ligny's lake. The throb of excitement shriveled and gave up the ghost.

In its stead tolled the meaning of my sister's presence here where Captain Ligny had fanned his hate against Hugh

Martin, Wilfrid Giles and Garrett Blair. Last Saturday, while I was just beginning to look for a way out for Ligny, Stella—and Dan and Edmund Martin too—already knew the score.

Leaving the hut to its desolation, I went outside to Stella and showed the sheet of quarto.

"This paper," I said, "and the plasticine board are what you came for. It appears it's necessary for me to go back to Canberra with you."

"So you've thought things out for yourself," Stella said. "A good thing for me, because you're a difficult fellow to reason with. But the word is *compulsory*, Sandy, rather than *necessary*."

"Tell me," I said after a pause, "what would have happened if I had not come here today?"

"You would have been summoned sooner or later. I'm sorry, Sandy," she said, the compassion back in her eyes.

"Does that mean I'm booked to be arraigned before the big brass?"

"Only Dan," said Stella. "But that's bad enough. . . ."

In our respective cars, we returned to Seymour, where the Marchmonts in their hospitable fashion lodged Stella for the night. A little after two-thirty the next afternoon, August 22, I sat listening to my brother-in-law in his sumptuous living room, which overlooked Ligny's garden, burgeoning in the early springtime sun. Far different, I reminded myself, from the scene of the previous Saturday when the garden had writhed under the gale from the Snowy Mountains and two policemen had skulked among the shrubs.

Dan and I were alone. Stella was resting, recuperating from the last two strenuous days, but I also gathered she was of the opinion that Dan and I would talk more freely and frankly on our own. That was Dan's opinion, too. He voiced it as he was pouring whiskey for both of us, and his tone gave rise to the reflection he had asked Stella to keep out of the way.

A demimillimeter of shift in chin, lips, nose and eyes up or down or sideways and you have a stranger in front of you. Still urbane, still the discreet, elegant, sagacious, important official, Dan was now a stranger. He placed my whiskey before me, took his own drink to the opposite side of the table, sat down and surveyed me. I decided the light in his blue eyes was like the cold, impersonal light of a mercury vacuum lamp.

"Well, let me hear the worst," I said.

The lines biting in around his nose and mouth, he began by informing me I was a bloody nuisance and a fool as well. I had refused to pay any heed to warnings, and if I hadn't been Stella's brother, he would have let me take the reward of thick-witted oafs. As it was—

He leaned his elbows on the table and wagged a forefinger. He had to remind me, he said, that he worked in the Attorney General's Department. Perhaps I also apprehended that the Attorney General's Department had, among its many functions, the administration of the Australian Security Intelligence Organization. He, Dan, was the officer who maintained liaison between the Attorney General and the A.S.I.O.

"In other words, you're a part of Security," I said, interrupting the harangue.

He allowed that in a sense that was correct and just as well for me it was. Last Saturday, there had been, apart from Lewis Ligny himself, seven individuals who knew Ligny had *not* drowned at Batemans Bay. He identified these seven individuals—Sandy Carmichael, Stella, Dan himself, the Prime Minister, the Attorney General, Colonel Hansen, the director of A.S.I.O., and Edmund Martin, the second in command. . . .

Dan broke off at this point. "Is there anything bothering you, laddie?" he asked coldly.

I *was* bothered. The news that the highest government echelons were concerned with Ligny was a staggerer, but it was the disclosure of Martin's position in A.S.I.O. that gripped my attention, and I rapidly reviewed the events of last Saturday. I recalled that Martin had left Ligny's place immediately after morning tea, thereby allowing himself

89

plenty of time to catch an earlier plane to Melbourne than the one I traveled in. He had had time to search my motel suite—but not enough time to get away before I myself had arrived, and so he laid me out cold. I decided that one of these days I would have to plug Edmund Martin in his ugly jaw.

"My mind wandered," I said to Dan, who was eyeing me disapprovingly. "What were you saying?"

"I'm talking to you for your own good," Dan said, "so keep your mind on the job."

He resumed his discourse. As he had already said, last Saturday there had been seven people who knew Ligny was still alive. Now, because of my barging in where I had no right or justification to be, the number had increased to nine, possibly ten. By barging in, he did not mean my seeing Ligny at Festival Hall or my reporting the occurrence. What he did refer to was my actions subsequent to my return to Melbourne with the result that two more individuals, maybe three, knew the secret of Ligny.

"I'll name them," Dan said. "The certainties are Miss Rhoda Hancock of Mount Worriong and Malcolm Blair, alias Red Aherne, the pugilist, of Mahon's Crossing. The doubtful person is John Morgan, the sporting writer."

He paused to savor my dismay.

"We're not fools in Canberra, laddie," he said. "We even know you stole a book from Ligny's study last Saturday— Thoreau's *Walden*. And we know why you took it, too. What did you tell Morgan the journalist?"

Damn Edmund Martin and his snooping! I had no call to feel guilty. Flustered and embarrassed, yes, but with no sense of guilt. Yet, like a peccant schoolboy bowled out, I found myself lamely explaining that my dealings with Morgan comprised merely asking for the true name of Red Aherne.

"Would you swear to that?" Dan demanded like a judge distrustful of a quailing witness.

"Yes," I said. Then I felt my face burn. I was no petty crook. There was no criminal offense in striving to help a man I had considered a friend. "Yes," I said angrily. "And to hell with you, Dan."

"You don't really understand the position yet," said Dan, unperturbed. "Let me explain it plainly and clearly. I can take your word for Morgan, so there are nine people who know the truth of Ligny's disappearance. We know that eight of them will not talk. You're the weak link, Sandy, with your traipsing around the country asking for Ligny. If the truth about him ever gets out, the press, white, pink or yellow, will have a week of field days, and heads will roll, high and low, and the first will be yours. Do you want the big guns of A.S.I.O. on your back?"

Now I did understand.

"You can imagine the furor," Dan went on, "if the news is published that a highly classified government job was held down by a murderer and the murderer has disappeared."

A little breeze stole through the window, bearing the scent of the flowers in Ligny's garden and evoking a picture of the marred face I had watched bending over the little lake in the annex. I stood up to get more whiskey.

"You're pretty certain of yourself," I said, dropping back into my chair.

Surprisingly adopting a conciliatory tone, Dan said he and Stella understood and sympathized with my feelings for Ligny. They had also regarded Ligny as a friend. He had been their neighbor for years, and they had liked him immensely, but what could you do when you discovered a friend to be a foul, murdering hypocrite?

At least, I said to myself, you can listen to what could be said on his behalf. Aloud I said, "What precisely did Ligny do?"

"I don't know the precise details," said Dan. "And I don't want to know. But I rather suspect from your recent activities you know all about it yourself."

"Was it Edmund Martin who started the probe into Ligny?"

"It's his job, laddie."

"Would you care to tell me how long he has been stationed here in Canberra?"

"I don't know if it's a matter of your business," Dan said, "but Ted Martin has been here about three months."

"And before that?"

"Various assignments in restricted areas around the country."

It all fits in, I reflected; Martin was a relative of Hugh, probably a brother, and he was impelled less by the need of government security than by his own personal animus.

"You have stated I have to understand the situation," I said. "So far you've kept to what you call the underground investigation into Ligny. But I suppose there *is* some kind of public investigation. After all, Ligny's disappearance was publicly announced."

Dan stood up, went to a sideboard, picked up a copy of the Canberra *Times* and put it in front of me, opened at the third page.

"See for yourself," he said, resuming his seat.

I read a brief account of a coroner's inquiry at Batemans Bay into the disappearance of Mr. Lewis Ligny while fishing from rocks nearby. After hearing evidence that Mr. Ligny's car and fishing gear had been found, the coroner, moralizing over the loss of a valuable citizen and uttering a strong warning against inexperienced people fishing from dangerous rocks, stated there were no suspicious circumstances and he adjourned the court *sine die* to enable the Batemans Bay police to prosecute further search for the body.

"No body will be found, of course," Dan said. "And Ligny will not argue when eventually he is legally deemed to be dead."

I did not venture into the questions raised by the latter portion of Dan's dictum.

"What is happening to the house and furniture?" I asked.

"So far, no will has been found and no relatives located.

So my department has put an auditor into the house to list the effects. As well, they have appointed a trustee." Dan leaned back in his chair. "I am the trustee," he said.

"Very neat and tidy," I said.

I thought of the probable fate of Ligny's lake—dismantled and the unsalable pieces dumped into a rubbish tip. There was nothing I could do to preserve an icon.

Straightening up, my brother-in-law resumed his magisterial mien, and I braced myself for another buffet. He unwrapped the packet that contained the quarto sheet and the plasticine board. These, he said, were confirmation of a report already received, and if I was interested—Dan read my mind—in why Stella was the courier to Mick's Hollow, the reason was that there had been nobody else to send. Moreover, if I wanted to know the particulars of the "report already received," I could only want—I wouldn't be told.

"Though I give you credit for these items," Dan continued, nodding at the board and the graph-cum-Merino-like map, "you've been holding out on me, laddie. I refer to the third item you found in the Hancock hut. Stella said you put it in your wallet."

No wonder Stella thought that Dan and I were better off on our own. I swore fiercely and fervently, but I got out my wallet and tossed the innocuous birthday card in front of Dan.

"There it is," I said. "And you know what you can do with it."

As Dan read the inscription, his black scowl slowly faded.

"Well, well!" he said. " 'To Uncle Mick, from your loving grandnephew, Wesley. From one misfit to another.' This is intriguing, laddie, because it supports the story the Hancocks were a turbulent crowd. Old Mick Hancock was mad, and as for this fellow Wesley, he was an outlaw. He got into all sorts of trouble, and in the end his father kicked him out. There wasn't much weeping when he went off to the war. But you'd know this already—" Dan stopped and eyed me sharply. "Why *did* you save this relic?"

93

Another straw to the camel-load of Edmund Martin's sniffing on my trail. I felt sick.

"I found it intriguing the same way as you," I said. "But that was all."

Dan pushed the card back to me.

"Ah, well," he said, "I'm glad—really glad it's not important. Tear it up or keep it and hang it in a frame in your caravan; it doesn't matter. And now . . ."

He waited as I replaced the card in my wallet.

"Now, laddie," he said. "I take it I can report to the higher-ups there'll be no more bother from you. After this, thought of Ligny will be locked into the oblivion of unmentionable things. But if you've got something still on your mind, now is the chance."

There was one point, a small point and perhaps irrelevant now—the question of Miss Hancock's copy of *Walden,* which had stood for years on Ligny's shelves, seemingly untouched and unread. Yet Ligny had been a student of Thoreau. Had there been another copy of *Walden* in Ligny's possession?

"I'd like a last look inside Ligny's place," I said.

Dan laughed in his old genial way.

"No worries," he said. "If you want a final chance to play with trains and boats, it's all right with me. Just let me tell Stella where we're going."

We emerged onto the footpath, strolled the few paces to Ligny's side gate and descended through the garden to the front porch. The housekeeper, Mrs. Jeffries, met us at the front door, and we passed through the hall into the transverse passage. Dan went to turn left to the way out to the annex, but I turned right toward the den.

"I want to see the books," I said.

We entered the study and I looked over the desks and worktable and cabinet and racks of instruments and shelves of books. A dark-headed man was working at the worktable with a sheaf of papers.

"My brother-in-law, Sandy Carmichael," Dan said to the

man. "A friend of the late Mr. Ligny. Sandy, meet Mr. Pemberton, our auditor."

We exchanged handshakes, and Pemberton said, "I guess you know this room well, Mr. Carmichael."

"Very well," I said.

The auditor gave his head a mournful shake. "Very unfortunate," he said, "that a man like Mr. Ligny should be drowned fishing—tragic."

"Have you listed all the books?" I asked, moving along the shelves and very conscious that Dan was watching me. This time I wouldn't get a chance to help myself to one of Ligny's books.

"Just about," Pemberton said. "It's been a tedious job."

"Did you happen to run across a copy of Thoreau's *Walden?*"

Pemberton gave me a curiously searching glance.

"As a matter of fact, I did find a copy of *Walden,* though not in here. Mr. Ligny kept it by his bedside—apparently one of his favorite books. But it's not there now."

"Where is it then?"

Pemberton looked inquiringly at Dan, and Dan nodded.

"An old lady called Miss Hancock came on Wednesday and got the book," said Pemberton. "She had written authority from Mr. Martin—do you know him, Mr. Carmichael?—and so I had no reason or right to say her no."

I swung round to stare at Dan.

"What about the annex?" he said gently.

I deduced from his face he judged he had driven the last nail into the coffin of my hopes for Ligny. And at first, with my knowing Miss Hancock had irrevocably aligned herself against me, that seemed the case. Then I saw in a burst of inspiration that the great unconformity of Ligny's life leapt into life again—or rather, the path to resolve it in my favor.

I took care to dissemble my feelings.

"I don't think I'm inclined now to potter round with trains," I said to Dan. "The best thing for me is to get back to Seymour as fast as I can. . . ."

8

Next morning I woke up in the caravan to the music of magpies warbling in the red gums along the river. The sun patterned the park with level corridors of amber, the wattles dappled the hills with gold and green, the smell of spring was in the air, and there was a bustle of caravans going and coming.

I had the sensation of having escaped from a black tunnel peopled by grisly shapes. Wherever Ligny was, whatever he was doing, I had regained my vision of him, had recovered the conviction he was not a murderer and, if there had been deception on his part, its intent was not evil.

Hurrying through showering, shaving and breakfasting, I went to Len Marchmont's office to test an assumption arising out of Miss Hancock's visit to Ligny's place in Canberra. I put a telephone call to Worriong Cottage to be told by Mrs. Riley that Miss Hancock was still away, "traveling." My guess was correct. Wherever Miss Hancock was traveling, it would be with Edmund Martin's cognizance and sanction and direction.

All the more need for fast work, Carmichael.

Back in the fo'c'sle, I settled down with pencil and paper to make a schedule of events. Not merely the events I could attest to but also those I could only surmise, and where I couldn't surmise, enter a query. I finished up with a rough diary.

Fri., Aug. 15

Ligny disappears at Batemans Bay.
I see him at night in Festival Hall.
I telephone Dan.

Sat., Aug. 16

I fly to Canberra; meet Dan, Stella, Martin; pinch *Walden*.
Martin flies to Melbourne—say, 1 P.M.
I fly back to Melbourne 2:30.
Martin knocks me out—say 4:30.

Sun., Aug. 17

I put in day studying *Walden*.
Martin visits Malcolm Blair at Mahon's Crossing.

Mon., Aug. 18

I restore *Walden* to Miss Hancock at Worriong Cottage.
Return to town and talk to John Morgan.
Martin—?

Tues., Aug. 19

Martin breaks into caravan, very early A.M.
I go from town to Mahon's Crossing, interview Malcolm Blair, then proceed to Seymour to view the damage to the caravan.
Martin visits Miss Hancock?
Miss Hancock starts interstate trip?

Wed., Aug. 20

I spend day in fo'c'sle reviewing situation. Ring Worriong Cottage to learn Miss Hancock away, interstate.

97

Miss Hancock calls at Ligny's home in Canberra; gets, on Martin's authority, the bedside copy of *Walden*.
Martin—?

Thurs., Aug. 21

I go to Mick's Hollow, find Stella there, return with her to Seymour.
Miss Hancock—?
Martin—?

Fri., Aug. 22

I go with Stella to Canberra, hold session with Dan and return to Seymour.
Miss Hancock—?
Martin—?

Sat., Aug. 23 (today)

I am in fo'c'sle, conducting thinkfest.
Miss Hancock not back at Worriong Cottage—but where?
Martin—?

Now, with the schedule in front of me, the inspiration kindled in Ligny's den yesterday hardened into sure understanding of events. The key was Miss Hancock's turning up at Ligny's place on Wednesday and confiscating the bedside copy of *Walden*—on the written authority of Martin.

I could see Martin arriving at Worriong Cottage on Tuesday, telling Miss Hancock who and what he was and why he was on Ligny's trail. Discovering Martin's sentiments to be identical with hers, Miss Hancock would display two exhibits—her diary and her *Walden*, relating how the latter had vanished from Worriong Cottage twenty-eight years earlier and she'd had no idea where it was until Sandy Carmichael, stating he had stolen the book from Ligny's shelves, had restored it to her only yesterday.

Then the fat would be in the fire. I couldn't imagine Martin confessing he had already seen the book in my pocket in the motel room on Saturday evening; if he had, Miss Hancock would have known it was he who knocked me cold, and I didn't think Miss Hancock would have appreciated that. But she and Martin would compare Thoreau's plan of Walden Pond with Miss Hancock's drawing of the half-starved sheep and then correlate both to the shape of Ligny's lake.

At this point, Martin, who had searched Ligny's house, would remember the bedside copy. Maybe he examined the book and found marginal notes, marked paragraphs, underlined sentences. This must have been the case, for there was no other reason for Miss Hancock to go to Canberra armed with Martin's authority to acquire the bedside copy.

And while Miss Hancock was occupied with her mission, what was Martin doing? Looking, I reasoned in reply, for the interpretation of Ligny's lake.

Immediately I knew I was wrong. As soon as Martin saw the likeness in the half-starved sheep, the plan of Walden Pond and Ligny's lake, he would understand. He had been after Ligny for months, perhaps years. He would have pried into Ligny's life from date of birth to date of alleged death. Long ago, he would have studied Captain Ligny's army record, and he wouldn't need any interpretation of Ligny's lake. After interviewing Miss Hancock at Worriong Cottage, he would in the very nature of things return to Mahon's Crossing to conscript Malcolm Blair in the campaign against Ligny, and Blair would not require much conscripting.

I had wasted six days, I thought. I had had the game in my grasp when I spent Sunday studying Miss Hancock's copy of *Walden*. Instead of chasing off to Mount Worriong and Mahon's Crossing, I should have stayed at the motel and read and reread *Walden* until it yielded up the secret of Ligny's lake.

Six days late, I thought, six days. I reached for my copy of *Walden*, put it on the desk and looked at it. My copy was no fine example of the bookbinder's craft. It was printed on cheap paper and bound in utilitarian green cloth and it had no portrait of Thoreau or plan of the pond. It was larger in print and page size than Miss Hancock's copy, running to 28 pages of introduction and 336 pages of text, whereas Miss Hancock's copy (I recalled) had 16 pages of introduction and 350 pages of text.

I remembered too that in Miss Hancock's copy Thoreau's plan of Walden Pond was on page 300, not far after the opening of the chapter "The Pond in Winter." The plan was important. Why shouldn't the text adjacent to the plan be just as important?

I did not need a slide rule to calculate that page 300 in Miss Hancock's copy would approximate to page 284 or 285 in mine. I opened my copy at page 285, turned the leaves back to the start of the chapter "The Pond in Winter," on page 281, began to read and kept on going to Thoreau's account of how he had measured and sounded the pond.

As I was desirous to recover the long lost bottom of Walden Pond, I surveyed it carefully, before the ice broke up, early in '46, with compass and chain and sounding line.

I was certain this sentence appeared halfway down page 289 in Miss Hancock's copy, the reverse of the page that carried the plan. But I paused before venturing on to the next one and a half pages. What was I seeking? The sound of Thoreau's voice or the echoes of Ligny's voice in response? I could not name it; yet I thought I would recognize it when I heard it.

I went on reading. First, Thoreau's observations on the credulous people who believed that "Walden (Pond) reached quite through to the other side of the globe," and the other people, just as credulous, who maintained that "a load of hay . . . if there were anybody to drive it," could be driven down to the source of the Styx and the entrance to the Infernal Regions.

Next, Thoreau's common sense displayed in fathoming the pond with "a cod-line and a stone weighing a pound and a half." (He found the greatest depth to be 102 feet.) Then I arrived at his conclusion that "probably the depth of the ocean will be found to be very inconsiderable compared with its breadth," and here I halted.

I had read a little over two pages following the statement that he had surveyed the Pond "early in '46," and I hadn't detected even a whisper. Where were the echoes of Ligny's voice replying to Thoreau's? I damned my lack of imagination, but I continued reading to where Thoreau, after mapping the pond, had discovered the line of greatest length intersected the line of greatest breadth "*exactly* at the point of greatest depth."

I said to myself, who knows but this hint would conduct to the deepest part of the ocean as well as of a pond or puddle? Is not this the rule also for the height of mountains regarded as the opposite of valleys?

A bell tolled—or rather Thoreau's voice intoned: Mountains are the opposite of valleys. What is the opposite of lakes? And remembering the ribbed model on the plasticine board, I broke free from the shackles I had unwittingly confined myself in by concentrating upon mainland enclosures.

The islands of the sea was the answer. But which island and where?

Now I was right out on my own, far beyond the reach of Thoreau's voice. And far beyond the resources I had in the caravan, the various atlases and the bundle of road maps I had accumulated. What I needed was in the purveyors in Melbourne who dealt in Admiralty charts and army ordnance surveys. My watch showed the hands pointing to twelve o'clock. Plenty of time, I thought; then I remembered today was Saturday; before I could race down to the city, all business places would be closed and stay closed until Monday morning.

A weekend of impotent fretting while Martin was hard on Ligny's heels? Intolerable, and so, in desperate shift, I bearded

Len Marchmont in his office and asked him whether by some miracle I could find Admiralty charts in Seymour.

Len's blunt honest face sagged with astonishment.

"Admiralty charts!" he said. "What on earth do you want with Admiralty charts? You're miles from the sea."

"I need a chart—the right chart—to work out a problem."

Len contemplated me curiously.

"You know, Sandy," he said, "Beth and I are rather worried about you. It's not our business, of course, but—well, you've dropped your work and you've been tearing around the country. Not like you, Sandy. If there's any trouble, I might be able to help."

"There is trouble, but it's not mine," I said. "It belongs to a friend, and that is all I can tell you. But thanks all the same."

"Well, you know where we are, Beth and I," Len said. "But for Admiralty charts, I might be able to put you on to the right man, a fellow called Knox Gemmell."

"The local stationer?"

"Lord, no. He's one of the local teachers, but he's done a lot of ocean yachting in his time—the Sydney-to-Hobart race and that sort of thing. He could have Admiralty charts. I'll give him a ring and find out."

He reached for the telephone. Two minutes later, he replaced the receiver and said, "Knox will be expecting you right after lunch. Make it one-thirty sharp because he and his wife have a social engagement in the city for four o'clock."

Obeying Len's instructions, I drove through Seymour's outer hillside streets to a big tree-shaded home overlooking the river. Mrs. Gemmell, a pleasant middle-aged woman, met me at the front door and conducted me along a passage to a room that somewhat resembled Ligny's den: there were books, desk, worktable and a large square wooden cabinet furnished with shallow drawers.

I estimated Knox Gemmell to be about fifty years old.

Slightly above average height, broad-shouldered and strong, he had a high-domed head, very bright blue eyes and florid clean-cut features. He looked like an outdoor man, as a yachtsman should, and he also looked like a teacher.

We shook hands.

"I gather from Len Marchmont you want to look at Admiralty charts," he said in a firm, clear voice. "Australian charts, I presume. Well"—he indicated the wooden cabinet—"those drawers are full of them. Which ones do you want?"

I liked his tone, his manner, his directness, and I wished for an opportunity to yarn with him and discover how a man of his background came to be a country schoolmaster. But there was no time for that, and I produced my pocketbook with its outline of a one-legged Merino ewe.

"I'm looking for the chart that shows an island with this shape," I said. "I don't know where it is. It could be anywhere in the world, though I hope it's in Australian waters."

Mr. Gemmell's blue eyes registered astonishment.

"You amaze me, Mr. Carmichael," he said. "You really do. Do you know how many Admiralty charts are in existence?"

"A lot, I suppose."

"I don't know the exact number myself, Mr. Carmichael, but it runs into many tens of thousands, and it would be a colossal job to look through every one of them." Mr. Gemmell paused to study my outline. "But that's not the reason for my amazement. What does startle me is quite another matter."

He went to the cabinet, pulled out a drawer and after a little searching, chose a chart and placed it on the worktable.

"Look at this, Mr. Carmichael," he said, and he pointed at a one-legged Merino shape occupying the middle of the chart.

"If you look in the *Nautical Gazetteer* there," Mr. Gemmell went on, nodding at the bookshelves, "you would read, 'Coupe Island, Bass Strait; uninhabited; muttonbirds; 39 19

103

S, 149 51 E.' I wouldn't dare to claim this outline hasn't been duplicated somewhere in the world—perhaps repeated half a dozen times; but you must come seeking an island—*this* island on which, for my sins, I had to live for a while. Now you understand my amazement."

In this chart, Coupe Island was the only visible land form in a waste of sea. I had to turn the chart sideways to get the true aspect of a sheep, for the long axis pointed nearly to north and south. According to the scale, the island had a length of two miles and, at its greatest breadth, it was about one mile. Just where one could expect to see the eye of the sheep was a hatched cone enclosing the figures 350′—quite an eminence for a small island—but the rest of it was blank except for the printed name.

39 19 South, 149 51 East? I visualized a map of Bass Strait. Coupe Island should be in the region of the Furneaux Group, say eighty miles slightly north of east from Flinders Island. It would be no easy job to get to Coupe Island.

"You say, Mr. Gemmell, the place is uninhabited?" I said.

"Deserted is the better word, except the sea birds and the muttonbirds hatching their young in spring," Mr. Gemmell said. "Please sit down, Mr. Carmichael—that is, if you have the time to hear a story."

It was obvious Mr. Gemmell had forgotten the social engagement in the city and I didn't remind him of it. Seating ourselves, we lit our pipes and Mr. Gemmell embarked into a story that, in some aspects, had remarkable similarities to the story of Captain Ligny, W.O. Martin and Sergeants Giles and Blair.

"At the beginning of 1942," Mr. Gemmell said, "I was a corporal in an A.I.F. battalion in the Kimberleys in W.A. One day I was pulled out and sent back to Royal Park to take part in a course not made clear to me at the time. If I'd known what was in store, I'd have fought like fury to get out of it. But I didn't know, and at Royal Park I met four other men who had to undergo the course, too—a major, a lieutenant and a couple of sergeants. The major, a fellow called Edwards, apparently knew what was happening, but he said the rest of us would have the knowledge dawn slowly on us as the course progressed—at least, he said he hoped so."

Mr. Gemmell laughed.

"It dawned all right. I won't go into the details—the torturing physical training, the brain work, the weaponry practice, the experiments with explosives and so on. The one redeeming feature was we were in the circumstances a happy bunch. I suppose the credit should go to the major—Major Edwards. He had a sense of humor—mostly sardonic. I'll always remember my first try at delousing a mine—a harmless mine, and just as well. My hand slipped and Major Edwards, standing over me, said, 'Gemmell, you've just sent me winging up to the pearly gates.' 'What about me, sir?' I asked, and he said, 'You're just landing in hell for making such a bloody awful blue.'"

Mr. Gemmell laughed again. I laughed, too, and then I reminded him of Coupe Island.

"I'm sorry," he said. "I'm wandering. As I said, the light dawned on us slowly. Some high-up expert decided the war would last a long time and the army needed specialists in destruction—massive destruction at the cost of a few expendable lives. We, and others like us, were the expendables and Coupe Island was the last stage in our training, and the most dangerous. That was why the army picked out Coupe Island. It was lonely. Fishermen never went there. It was well off the steamer lanes and civil aircraft flew well away from it and if we blew ourselves up, which was on the cards every day, there was no one to talk about it. You understand, of course, we were sworn to secrecy."

"Were there any accidents?"

"Not with our lot," Mr. Gemmell said. "There were whispers about other contingents, though we never heard the details. Just as well, too. Morale, Mr. Carmichael."

I was almost on the tip of asking if Mr. Gemmell had heard

the name of Captain Ligny, but in the nick of time I altered the question.

"Mr. Gemmell, did you ever meet or hear of other men training on the island—that is, besides your own people?"

"Not to my knowledge," said Mr. Gemmell. "Each lot going to Coupe Island was self-contained and isolated. We weren't told who had preceded us or would be following us and we were warned never to make any inquiry." He put a match to his pipe, "You know, Coupe Island was where I got the itch for yachting."

"Is that so?"

"Yes. As well as playing around with explosives and crawling blindfolded through live minefields and dodging flamethrowers and studying the art of sabotage in a big way, we were also trained in managing small vessels—canoes, dinghies, launches, yachts. That was how I became a yachtsman after the war."

"What happened to you after you left Coupe Island?"

The usual thing, Mr. Gemmell said. One of the sergeants was killed in Timor when they blew up an aviation petrol dump; the young lieutenant disappeared during a night raid on shipping in Singapore, and the second sergeant died in a similar raid at Hollandia. After that, Mr. Gemmell and the major, joining a group called "Z" Force, finished up in Borneo behind the Japanese lines. From there, when the war had ended, they returned to Melbourne, the major to die in the Repatriation Hospital and Mr. Gemmell to resume his teaching studies in the college from which he had enlisted at the outbreak of war, and to indulge his liking for yachting.

"Expendable," I said.

"It's a long time ago," Mr. Gemmell said. He turned his bright blue eyes on me. "Back to the point, Mr. Carmichael. Why are you interested in Coupe Island—rather, in an island resembling Coupe Island?"

I knew that had to come and I knew, too, I could not brush the question off, not after Mr. Gemmell's courteous response

106

to my request. I pondered for a moment my brother-in-law's warnings; then, damning the consequences, I decided I could confide in Mr. Gemmell without divulging Ligny's name.

"I'm looking for a friend who's disappeared," I said. "It happened in another state, so you wouldn't see much reference to it in Victorian newspapers, but the official opinion is he was accidentally drowned in the sea. I wasn't satisfied and I believe he voluntarily disappeared. I have looked through his effects and I came across certain papers which make me think he has run away to a secret hideout. Now I've seen this chart, I'm convinced he has gone to Coupe Island, and somehow I've got to get there myself."

Mr. Gemmell subjected me to a long cool stare.

"This is a remarkable story," he said.

"You really mean incredible. But I assure you it is true."

"Len Marchmont told me you were an engineer," Mr. Gemmell said. "You are not a detective?"

"I am an engineer, Mr. Gemmell."

"Sure there's no smell of police matters?"

"Mr. Gemmell, I could produce evidence that a coroner's inquiry found there were no suspicious circumstances in the affair. But I don't want to produce the evidence because of regard for my friend. I want to keep his name from public notice."

I saw a slight relaxing of Mr. Gemmell's manner.

"Was your friend mentally disturbed?" he asked.

"Not mentally disturbed," I said, "but he was disturbed. Unfortunately, he kept his worries from his friends, but he wasn't out of his mind."

"How old is your friend— No," Mr. Gemmell said quickly with a hint of a smile, "I can't ask that. But it doesn't stop me thinking he's about my age, old enough, like me, to have sharp memories of a place like Coupe Island. No, Mr. Carmichael"—he held up a hand at me—"no need to go into that. You want to get to Coupe Island. Any idea of how you'd get there?"

"No idea at all, except, having looked at the chart, I might fly down to Flinders Island and persuade a fisherman to ferry me from there."

Mr. Gemmell shook his head.

"I don't know I should favor that," he said. "There might be another way—" Again he appraised me. "You're really determined to go to Coupe Island?"

"I am."

"Do you know what you would be in for?"

"I've had some experience of roughing it. I've also been in the army."

"I didn't mean that," he said.

He stood up and started back and forth along the length of the room and now I understood he was debating whether he should help me or thank me for a dubious story and show me out. In his eyes, I could almost see the decision going against me when there was a deprecatory throat-clearing and I looked around to see Mrs. Gemmell in the doorway.

"I'm sorry I have to intrude," she said. "But, Knox, have you forgotten the time? We're due in the city by four o'clock, remember."

Mr. Gemmell stopped in his tracks.

"Oh, Lord! I *had* forgotten. Mr. Carmichael, we've got to go. We have the most important function in town—our grandson's fourth birthday party. If you don't mind, we'll have to shoo you off. . . . Get the car out, dear," he said to his wife. "I'll be with you in a moment."

He went to the desk, scribbled a few furious lines on a slip of paper, folded the slip and tucked it in an envelope. He wrote a name on the envelope and handed it to me.

"Do you happen to know anything about Port Connal?" he asked.

"I've driven through it on the way to Wilson's Promontory."

"Good," said Mr. Gemmell. "Go to Port Connal, hunt up Amos Waller and give him this note. He's a fisherman, as you may guess, and he can get you to Coupe Island. You can rely on him and he'll not overcharge you. More importantly, he's no blabbermouth. . . ."

I have never been able to decide, subsequently, who was actually responsible for my introduction to Amos Waller, fisherman—Mr. Gemmell, Mrs. Gemmell or their grandson celebrating his fourth birthday that day.

9

At 4:45 A.M. the following Tuesday, under a westering moon, Amos Waller set me down on a tiny strip of shingly beach at the northernmost tip of Coupe Island. I surveyed the immediate scene in the beam of the searchlight of Waller's trawler, the *Wee Anne*, lying out half a cable's length in the flat dark sea, and then I looked up beyond the cliff at a dim shape silhouetted against the southern stars. In the weak moonlight, I had an impression of a monstrous black pyramid reaching into the sky. I shivered in my duffle coat, though I knew the pyramid was only the hillock I had seen marked on Mr. Gemmell's chart.

Waller, a blond, thickset man in heavy jersey and corduroy trousers and gumboots, said gruffly, "You're sure you've got everything?"

I surveyed my two packs; one holding rations, spare clothing, towels, soap, matches, first-aid kit, a bottle of whiskey, a small flask also full of whiskey; the other a pup tent wrapped around a sleeping bag, inflatable mattress, tobacco, cooking pots, small Primus stove, can of kerosene, bottle of methylated spirits, a battery-powered lamp. My binoculars rested against the second pack and, beside them, a knapsack containing a battery-operated shaver and a parcel of spare batteries for the shaver and the lamp. Then I checked my pockets —pipe, more tobacco, more matches, handkerchiefs, pencils, notebook, wallet, clasp knife, torch and extra batteries.

"I've got everything," I said, and I shivered again, but this time from the chill of the Bass Strait air.

"For a start, there's a steep pinch up the cliff," Waller said in his growling tone. "About a hundred feet, and be careful near the top. The granite is old and rotten and you could fall through a muttonbird burrow. Last time I was here years ago, I saw six wooden huts sou'east of the hill—old army huts, so I've heard. They might still be livable. Anyway, there's a spring of fresh water near the huts—or used to be. I guess you won't have to drink the sea."

"What about seafood?" I asked.

"This place isn't noted for fish or crays," Waller said. "That's why fishermen never come here. You might fancy a muttonbird when they come, though I wouldn't—too oily for me. But you're too early for the muttonbirds. Another two or three weeks before they're due."

"I won't be eating muttonbird early or late," I said.

Waller gave a hoarse chuckle.

"Well, so long, Mr. Carmichael," he said. "Expect me in ten days—Friday, September 5, about midday, give or take a few hours. And I hope you'll be ready."

We shook hands and Waller, getting into his dinghy, sculled back to the trawler. I saw him and his two crewmen hoisting the dinghy aboard. The engines began to throb, the kedge was raised, the searchlight winked out and the *Wee Anne* headed to the crayfish grounds ninety miles away. Waller played a honking farewell on the foghorn. The blasts bounced back from the cliffs and startled seabirds into wild flutterings and terrified outcries.

I watched until the *Wee Anne*'s lights had faded; then I

took my torch out and shone the beam up the cliff. Steep, but far from impassable. I shouldered the first pack, slung the binoculars and knapsack over my free arm and followed the torchlight up through the muttonbird burrows and out onto a plat of ground covered with wet waist-high bracken. Here I dumped my burdens and slid down the cliff for the second pack.

Once more on the top with all my belongings piled in the bracken, I lit my pipe and looked around. Now the monstrous pyramid had become what it actually was, a moderate hill wanly silvered by moonlight. The galaxy stretched overhead in faraway majesty and the night still held sway except for a small dull glow in the east.

I was the victim of Amos Waller's timetable and there was nothing I could do until daylight appeared. I slung the binoculars over my shoulder and, the torch showing the way, climbed through the bracken to the crest of the hillock, found a boulder of granite and sat down to wait for sunrise.

I thought of Ligny somewhere on this dark island and I thought of Martin, wondering whether he was behind me in the race or had already come and departed with his purpose accomplished. And then I thought of Mr. Gemmell's surprisingly gratifying introduction to Amos Waller.

"I commend Mr. Carmichael to you," Mr. Gemmell had written to Waller. "Mr. Carmichael, who combines engineering with natural history, wishes to observe wildlife in Bass Strait and I have suggested Coupe Island to him. Knowing you are often in the vicinity of Coupe Island, I have no doubt you will have little trouble in getting Mr. Carmichael to the island."

"Vicinity be damned!" Waller had growled when he read this missive at Port Connal on Sunday. "Knox Gemmell must be getting old. He knows the nearest I get to Coupe Island is ninety miles away. As for wildlife, there's more wildlife here in Port Connal than in all Bass Strait."

Nevertheless, Waller had undertaken to transport me to

Coupe Island, but I would have to await his pleasure, the tides and the weather. It had been Monday evening when I boarded the *Wee Anne* and in consequence it had been half-past three in the morning when Waller awakened me, fed me a breakfast of sausages and toast and hot tea and then landed on the shingly beach.

The cold began to creep into my bones. I jumped up from the granite, stamped around in the bracken and rubbed my hands together and tucked them into my armpits. All at once I became aware that day was at hand. The gloom cloaking the sea receded from the island, the stars faded and the moon, low down, had a sickly hue. The eastern glow broadened, a light wind stirred the bracken icily, and the seabirds—terns, silver gulls, big Pacific gulls, shearwaters—foraged along the cliffs and out to sea.

In the pallid presunrise light, I could pick out the dark form of Coupe Island against the sea and I had a start of surprise, though there shouldn't have been, in recognizing the one-legged Merino-like outline. And not only surprise, but also a wonder that my filching Thoreau's *Walden* had brought me ten days later to be standing here on this hillock, the center of a huge empty circle of water.

The six army huts mentioned by Amos Waller stood about four hundred yards from the hill, looking as though they had grown out of the bracken. A quarter of a mile southeast of the huts was the haunch of the cape that represented the ewe's one leg and I descried a series of ridges extending east and west across the island's width—the "ribs" of Miss Hancock's "half-starved sheep." I counted seven of them, but there could have been a couple more, out of sight at the south end of the island. From where I stood on the hill, it appeared that abrupt cliffs faced the sea in every direction, which stirred the question of where Ligny had harbored the vessel that must have carried him to Coupe Island. I let the question lie fallow.

113

In the ubiquitous bracken were signs of the army's long-gone occupation apart from the huts. There were traces of digging, little dips in the bracken as though it had grown in and over trenches. There were bracken-clothed mesa-like humps that could have been parapets or bunkers and I concluded after scrutiny through the binoculars that in the sides of the ridges were openings to dugouts or tunnels. These man-made scars would have to be examined close at hand.

Then I reminded myself again that Lewis Ligny was my goal, not curious sight-seeing. Once more I scanned the island for signs of life—movement, rustlings in the bracken, wisps of smoke from a cooking fire. For all I could see, I was alone on the island. The huts were silent and deserted. Only the seabirds moved in the field of vision. But, I told myself, Ligny had to be here.

I found the spring Waller had spoken of in a hollow, the water trickling away to the sea through a miniature bracken-choked gorge. It was a hundred yards from the nearest hut, the one on the east end of the line, and so I chose this hut as my headquarters. But there was no variation in the huts except in the matter of size. The hut on the west end was bigger and the hut next to it was smaller than the remaining four. Apparently the large hut had been a combined mess and recreation room, and the faded sign on the small hut told me it had been the orderly office.

The huts all faced eastward, their blank rear walls turned to wild weather. All dilapidated, they were the haunt of spiders, and the floors were a mess of sand and dead bracken fronds. I guessed that for cooking the army had used a field kitchen, which would have been taken away when the island was abandoned. But in the large hut I made two finds. First, an old straw broom; second, about three hundredweight of briquettes cached in a closed-in recess. There was no need, therefore, for me to go to bed cold.

Where, I asked myself, was Ligny camped?

I took the broom back to my hut, swept out the fronds and grit and removed the dead ashes from the fireplace. Then I carried my packs in. I was hungry, but I was also impatient to get on with the job of exploring Coupe Island. Accordingly, I emptied my pockets of the things I didn't need straightaway, opened a carton of chocolate emergency rations and broke out a slab to munch on the way. A drink of water at the spring, and I was ready.

To do the job thoroughly I should have traced an imaginary grid covering every few square yards, but that process would have taken me a fortnight, so I zigzagged down the island from side to side. I expected my progress to be slow, but it was slower than I had imagined because the thick bracken not only masked the man-made scars—the trenches, dugouts, saps, foxholes, water-logged tunnels—but it was a cover for great lengths of rusty barbed wire.

It was just as I would have pictured a long-deserted battlefield. In a cluster of mine craters and grenade pockmarks, I found my boot nudging a rusty Mills bomb. I jumped back smartly and eyed it nervously until I saw it had been deloused. And then I thought of Mr. Gemmell's description of how he and his companions had had to wriggle through live minefields. After that, I went very circumspectly. A live mine, even after twenty-eight years, would be no picnic for the person who trod on it.

I arrived at a depression toward the bottom end of the island where I thought I would walk without fear of treading on a mine, though I still had to look out for barbed wire lurking in the bracken. Though this area had its quota of trenches and bunkers, it was more notable for a great belt of bare granite showing the black and white glaze of heat. I felt sure this was where Mr. Gemmell and his party had played around with flamethrowers. And not only Mr. Gemmell's team but also Captain Ligny, W.O. Martin and Sergeants Giles and Blair.

Perhaps this was where Hugh Martin, Wilfrid Giles and Garrett Blair had died.

I continued south until I could go no farther, halting on the brink of a fierce cliff that curved northward on either side. There was no beach. The sun was warm on my back, but a cool southeasterly breeze blew, scarcely raising a ripple on the slumberous swell working in from the Tasman Sea.

Chewing the last of the chocolate, I surveyed the northern aspect, the succession of ridges culminating in the hillock two miles away. The cliff scarps were dark against the blue of the sea. I could see that some corners of the shoreline were out of sight to any watcher on the island itself and I wished I had a boat.

Damn it, Carmichael; what's your grief? Ligny is here—right here on the island where you should be able to see him. Or some sign of him.

After finishing the chocolate, I found I was thirsty and I searched for another spring. I found one a furlong or so along the southwestern cliff, and the water was sweet and cold. After drinking, I watched the flow of water, dribbling over the granite down to the sea, turned around—*and there was Ligny.*

Though I couldn't see his face, it had to be Ligny. He was mounting the second ridge from me, heading north. I put two fingers in my mouth and blew a shrill whistle, but he didn't pause or look back. I whipped the binoculars to my eyes just in time to see a big form clothed in big-rimmed hat, duffle coat and trousers; then he disappeared down the other side of the ridge.

I started to run, awkwardly because of the confounded bracken, but I made good ground on him. When I panted up the second ridge, he was only one ridge ahead—a mere three hundred yards away.

"Ligny!" I yelled. "Carmichael here, Ligny!"

He must have heard me, but he continued ahead steadily and dipped once more out of sight. I burst into a sprint, crashing recklessly through the bracken, and there was my downfall. One moment I was stretching out like a quarter-miler, the next I was gasping at the bottom of a dugout with my left leg trapped in barbed wire.

A minute passed before I could get my breath back. Then I extricated my leg from the barbed wire and counted up the score. On the credit side, my pipe was safe, my watch still ticking and my bones intact. On the debit side, my trousers were torn, my shin gashed, my ribs bruised and my binoculars smashed beyond repair. Worst of all, I had lost Ligny.

Cursing the barbed wire, I limped up the next ridge, following Ligny's spoor in the crushed bracken. Beyond the crest, I came again to the memorial to the flamethrowers that had once squirted fire on Coupe Island—the stretch of heat-fused granite. Here Ligny had blinded his tracks very effectively. There was no mark of his boots on the granite and I couldn't discover where and how he had left the stone. I ranged over and around the bare patch until I gave up in exasperation. For all I could see to the contrary, he could have dematerialized at the point his tracks ended.

I sat down on the granite and smoked my pipe while I considered the problem. The area in front of me was corrugated and latticed with trenches and traverses and embankments, all, of course, choked and blanketed with bracken. Somehow Ligny had managed to gain the cover of this maze and I would have to go down into it and creep along every trench and fosse. I didn't care for the prospect. I was tired and the stinging in my shin had built up into burning. Then a shadow came over the island and I looked up to see that the westering sun had gone behind a high gray layer of cloud.

Westering? I raised my watch and saw the time was four-sixteen. The day had dissolved away. I needed a wash, a change of clothes, a good feed and sulpha powder for the inflamed shin. Ligny would have to wait until tomorrow.

I heaved myself up to my feet, and then I saw Ligny again, topping a ridge a good half-mile away. Just as if, I thought foolishly, he had popped down into the earth here and popped up there.

"Ligny!" I shouted. "Ligny!"

This time he vouchsafed to hear me. He stopped and looked back, a small figure dark against the horizon. Now I did bemoan the loss of the binoculars. Nevertheless, I saw him raise his arm and wave several times toward the huts, after which he deliberately descended the farther side of the ridge.

Ignoring the pain in my shin, I began to run. In the next fifteen minutes, I glimpsed him twice more—once passing over a ridge (I was catching up to him), and when I was crossing over the final crest, he was rounding the corner of my hut.

He was safe, I thought; no need now to run myself into the ground, and I slowed to a sedate walk. Rounding the corner myself, I saw him leaning in the doorway, and then I stopped short. How the hell, I thought, staring at a fur-lined leather jacket and long yellow hair sprouting untidily under a blue beret, could I have seen a big hat and duffle coat through the binoculars?

Edmund Martin came forward smiling and said, "I trust we meet in friendship."

It was the smile hinting at superior knowledge and authority that hurt, not the realization I had lost the race. I recalled his suave manner in Ligny's den and I thought of the knockout blow in the motel and the ravage of my caravan.

"I owe you a plug in the jaw, Martin," I said. "And now you're going to get it."

I jumped at him, swinging my fist, and a big hand gripped my arm and swung me round, and I looked into the face of Malcolm Blair.

"You!" I said furiously. "Well, I'll take you on, too."

"What with?"

"Boots and all—"

There I went silent. Miss Hancock walked from the hut, her black eyes sparkling.

"Gentlemen, gentlemen!" she said. "No fisticuffs, please."

10

I suppose Miss Hancock saved me from the father of a hiding, but at the moment I could only rue the day I first met her. It was my own fault that she and Martin and Blair were on the island and I eyed her with no feeling of gratitude.

Besides, I was sweaty and clammy with the evening chill, my leg ached abominably and I was conscious of the gaping rent in my trousers. Miss Hancock affected to ignore my discomfiture. Clad in warm woolens, shod with stout shoes, a furry black hat perched jauntily on her white head, her skin pink and gold, she was as unconsciously self-possessed as when I saw her in the sunroom at Worriong Cottage.

"Gentlemen"—she addressed Martin and Blair—"we owe an explanation to Mr. Carmichael and we must also confer with him. So, Mr. Carmichael"—she turned to me—"would you please come down to our launch with us?"

"Where is your launch?" I asked ungraciously.

Miss Hancock pointed toward the throat of the island's Merino shape and said, "It's in a kind of cave, Mr. Carmichael. According to Mr. Martin, the army developed it years ago into a landing for small vessels. The cliff is steep, but the steps down it are safe."

"I'm sorry," I said, "but I don't want to visit your launch."

His hair highlighted by the sun peeping suddenly through the clouds, Blair shook his bronze head. Martin frowned, then resumed his derisive air. I would have loved to wipe that look off his face.

"We can offer you a hot shower," Miss Hancock said, "and antiseptic cream for the gash in your leg, and I could repair the tear in your trousers. Afterwards, some sherry and then a hot meal. Our galley is really fitted up, Mr. Carmichael."

I considered telling Miss Hancock I had my own rations and first-aid kit and needle and thread. But only for a moment. That would have been too uncouth. Yet I still smarted under the blow of having my plans badly disrupted. I wanted Ligny to myself. Moreover, I had just realized I *had* seen Ligny this afternoon, for Blair, like Martin, was wearing a beret and a leather lumber jacket, and so I knew where I had to start looking for Ligny.

In his irritating superior way, Martin understood what I was thinking.

"You've already seen Captain Ligny," he said. "Probably talked to him, too. We've got binoculars, Carmichael."

"All the more reason for discussion," Miss Hancock said. She spoke to the big pugilist. "Mr. Blair, would you be so kind as to fetch three—no, *four* folding chairs from the launch. Mr. Carmichael's quarters are rather meager in amenities." She smiled at me; then it was Martin's turn. "Please go to the hut you called the mess room and gather up a heap of briquettes to start a fire in Mr. Carmichael's hut."

They didn't like it, but they submitted to Miss Hancock's bidding and they departed, Blair to the east, Martin to the west.

"I want a quiet word with you, Mr. Carmichael," Miss Hancock said. "And a quick word, for they won't take long. Mr. Carmichael"—her large dark eyes were friendly—"please do get down from your high horse. After all, we're just as entitled to be on Coupe Island as you. Mr. Martin is here because of his brother. Mr. Blair is here because of his father, and I—"

She hesitated and I said, "Why are you here, Miss Hancock?"

"To represent Wilfrid Giles," she said. "There is no one else to stand up for him."

"It's a pity we're on opposite sides," I said (as I had said once before). "I stand up for Lewis Ligny."

"Don't be so sure I'm against you," Miss Hancock said. "When Mr. Martin was arranging our trip to Coupe Island last Friday, I wanted to invite you too. Do believe me, Mr. Carmichael, because it is true. I persuaded Mr. Martin and Mr. Blair to agree, but the trouble was we couldn't find you. We had no time to scour the country for you because we were scheduled to leave Batemans Bay next day—that was where Mr. Martin hired our launch."

I could believe Miss Hancock, but as for Martin? He had known—and how!—the way to my caravan.

"I like you, Mr. Carmichael," Miss Hancock went on. "I really do, and I was delighted when we discovered you on the island when we arrived here at midday. And not only delighted, but astonished too. How did you work out the way to Coupe Island, Mr. Carmichael?"

"By reading *Walden,* Miss Hancock."

"By reading— Now I understand. You found a map of Coupe Island in my copy of *Walden* and you didn't tell me. Oh, Mr. Carmichael!"

"There was *no* map of Coupe Island in your copy, Miss Hancock. But was there one in the bedside copy you took from Ligny's on Wednesday?"

Miss Hancock regarded me thoughtfully.

"You've been talking to your brother-in-law," she said. "There was a map in that copy, and that was why I went to Canberra, and I would have told you if there had been an opportunity. But I'm afraid, Mr. Carmichael, you are not telling quite the truth yourself."

"Miss Hancock, there was no map in your copy," I said urgently, and I went on to describe how I discovered the existence of Coupe Island. "That is the truth," I said.

"You're very clever," she said, her face brightening. "Very ingenious, Mr. Carmichael. Yes. And now back to the point. I *was* delighted to find you on the island. If we can't amalgamate, the least we can do is to be friends. So do say you'll come to the launch and join us there. We are not savages."

A fair gesture, I thought. I surveyed the cliffs and the seabirds, the slaty gray sea and the saffron-fringed clouds moving under the sun. Then I contemplated Miss Hancock and her perky hat flaunting defiance at her years. Indomitable, but fragile, her pink-gold skin transparent with age. Martin should have never let her come on this expedition, but now I was glad she was here.

Martin emerged from the messroom, his arms clasped around a great heap of briquettes which threatened to spurt out of his grip. Almost at the same moment, Blair came panting up over the cliff brandishing the folding chairs in his mighty fists. Good training for a heavyweight champion.

"You acquiesce, Mr. Carmichael?" Miss Hancock said softly.

"Yes-s-s," I said.

Miss Hancock waited until her messengers had arrived at the hut.

"I'm glad to say," she said, "Mr. Carmichael has changed his mind. He has consented to join us in the launch."

Blair raised the chairs, regarded them solemnly, sighed and lowered them again. As for Martin, he went into the hut, deposited the briquettes on the hearth and reappeared, rubbing briquette dust from his hands.

"There's no need then to light a fire?" he inquired smoothly.

"Not at the moment."

"And the chairs?" asked Blair in an aggrieved fashion.

"We can take them back," said Miss Hancock. "At least, three of them. We'll leave one here for Mr. Carmichael's use."

Blair slid one of the chairs over the threshold.

"We are ready when you are, Mr. Carmichael," said Miss Hancock.

"I have two things to say first," I said, and I faced Martin. "Last Friday, I had a very bad time with my brother-in-law in Canberra. I gather from Miss Hancock you've heard about it."

"I did hear something of it," Martin admitted.

"Well then, am I putting myself in danger of arrest by Security?"

"That," Martin said, "depends entirely on your cooperation with us here. It will be ventilated at Miss Hancock's round-table conference. What's the next item?"

"An apology, Martin. You know exactly what I mean."

"I understand perfectly, Carmichael. That also will be dealt with at the conference."

There was no sense in making a scene, so I went into the hut and dug out a supply of clean clothes.

The steps Miss Hancock had spoken of had been hewn out of dark rock in the south wall of a chasm that penetrated deeply into the cliffs. The steps slanted seaward for eighty feet or so, then turned just as sharply in the opposite direction. In the cavernous gloom, it was not until we neared the bottom that I saw the ocean-going diesel launch moored fore and aft between platforms carved out of the rock.

I helped Miss Hancock down to the landing and halted to study the launch. The white seventy feet of hull and super-structure rose and fell in the sluggish water, and I heard the soft humming of a generator. The launch slithered lightly against fenders that protected her from the stone. This was luxury and I wondered who was paying for it—Miss Hancock or Martin or the champion boxer or all three? Or was it Security who was picking up the tab?

Looking for the entrance to the inlet, I saw no opening, only a cliff edge silhouetted against a more distant wall, and Martin said, "The army worked efficiently here. This bay—if that's the word—is an offshoot from the main fiord. Even in rough weather, this place is safe. Malcolm, we want some light."

Blair clambered across a gangway onto the deck. He disappeared into a companion below the bridge and in a moment lights came on, both inboard and deckside, and the vessel's name appeared, picked out in illuminated letters along the bridge transom.

ERICA
Batemans Bay

Then I discovered that the yacht was not alone in the recess. Tethered farther in was a much smaller craft, an unpretentious yawl.

"Captain Ligny's boat," said Martin. "He can't escape with us in the way, unless he swims. But he had time before we arrived to move his supplies to some lair on the island. A little while ago I said a certain contingency depended on your cooperation. The location of Ligny's hideout is what I want to get from you."

"But I don't know—"

"Don't start debating now," he interrupted me. "Keep it for the roundtable conference. . . ."

The feeling of suspenseful foreboding smoldered in the background for a time. After showering in the *Erica*'s head and applying ointment to my shin and donning fresh clothes in one of the *Erica*'s cabins, I drank sherry with Miss Hancock and Martin and Blair in the yacht's elegant main saloon and sat down to eat. Blair had apparently constituted himself ship's chef and I had no complaints about his cooking.

The meal proceeded without incident. And then, the table

cleared and the galley squared off, Miss Hancock began repairs to the torn trousers (despite my protests), and Martin spread out a large relief map of Coupe Island. Immediately the suspense reared up. I looked at the Merino-like outline— the driving, besetting Merino shape—and I looked at the details. The cliffs. The northern hillock, shading into the first of the nine ridges traversing the island. The dark lines and cross-hatching that represented bunkers and trenches and tunnels made by the army a generation earlier. A labyrinth of military planning.

"The map might be old," I said, "but the paper and the printing are new."

"I had it photostatted in army archives a few days ago," Martin said.

There was a change in his manner. No longer suave, he had shed his irritating air of superior knowledge. He was cold and hard and deadly in earnest. And Blair showed a similar change in demeanor. Even Miss Hancock, bending over her needlework, had altered. Before dinner, she had donned a dark suit that accentuated her white hair and pink-gold skin, but she was far from the Miss Hancock I knew at Worriong Cottage, just as far from the Miss Hancock who had persuaded me to come down to the launch.

All three were Ligny's enemies.

"What about my apology?" I said to Martin. "My *double* apology?"

He gave a rough laugh.

"An explanation but no apology," he said. "I did knock you out in the Parkville motel and I did ransack your caravan. I made a mess of it to make it seem the work of vandals, though I didn't know you would guess I was responsible—"

"Easy," I broke in, seizing the chance for some dirty infighting. "All I had to do was to count up the swines I've met, and there it was."

"Do you want to listen?" he demanded angrily.

Miss Hancock did not glance up from her sewing, but Malcolm Blair glowered as he had when his wife announced the police were searching for me. The generator throbbed and the deck trembled over the water's slow swell as though responding to the turbulence in the saloon.

"Keep going," I said to Martin.

"I had to do it," he said. "Though I was sure why Captain Ligny faked his drowning, I could not rule out another reason, so I had to look into the possibility of official secrets being betrayed: he was privy to important classified projects. And I couldn't disregard that you were a partner in his intrigues—"

"Good God!" I said. "I'm the man who saw Lewis Ligny in Festival Hall and then rang Dan Hilary in Canberra as soon as I heard the news about Ligny."

Martin looked me straight in the eye.

"How could I know—rather, prove—your call to Canberra wasn't a pretty ploy to muddy the trail? Or to make yourself safe? Or to get inside authority to learn what Security was doing? So I had to search your motel and your caravan to answer two questions. Were you part of an espionage ring and did you know where to look for Ligny? And, by God! I was half right. You did know where Ligny had gone. The proof of that is you're here yourself."

"My being here," I said, "is proof I'm fighting for Ligny. Ask Miss Hancock for that. But here is something beyond my guessing powers. What happened to make Ligny fake the drowning at Batemans Bay?"

There was silence for the space of five heartbeats; then Martin banged his fist on the table.

"I told him he was a murderer," he said. "A triple murderer and that I was able to prove it. When he disappeared at Batemans Bay, I thought he had at last done the right thing and killed himself. But when your phone call came that night, I knew he was not only a murderer but a coward as well."

I had merely to look at Miss Hancock and Blair to know they both endorsed Martin's sentiments.

"Well," I said, "I know Ligny. He is *not* a murderer and *not* a coward."

"You know him!" said Martin. "You met him only enough to look at his books and play round with the toy in the annex. And what is that to compare with the people who have been suffering for twenty-eight years because of him? Listen, Carmichael, Captain Ligny killed three men here on Coupe Island. Garrett Blair, who was Malcolm's father; Hugh Martin, who was my brother; and Wilfrid Giles. And the proof is right in front of you."

He tapped the relief map of Coupe Island.

"Do you want the proof?" he asked.

The great unconformity loomed again, painted larger than ever. The blackness of the chasm outside seemed to invade the saloon and writhe around the bright lamps.

"I'll listen," I said.

I skip quickly over Martin's preamble, the story of his initial questioning of his brother's death, a questioning that had actually begun as a result of letters slipped out uncensored before the fatality. ("Just like my father," interjected Blair.) In those letters Martin's brother had spoken of Captain Ligny and his hatred for the men under him and had described Elspeth Hancock's part in defeating Captain Ligny's censorship.

("Just the same as my father's letters," said Blair, but Miss Hancock did not speak, though her fingers were idle as Martin talked of Elspeth.)

The names of Hancock and Mount Worriong had therefore become fixed in Martin's memory, and also the names of Giles and Blair, and so after he had joined the Security Service and gained some authority, he had looked into Captain Ligny's war record. One thing had led to another. To his astonishment, he had discovered that Captain Ligny was present when W.O. Hugh Martin, Sergeant Wilfrid Giles and Sergeant Garrett Blair had died—"accidentally"—in 1941.

He had been convinced then that Captain Ligny had killed the three men, and he had set out to find evidence.

"Do you know anything about Special Operations Services in the Second War, Carmichael?" he asked.

"I know Coupe Island was the final stage in training men for special service," I said.

"You know too much," Martin said, his eyebrows bristling. "You might be a security risk after all."

"Get on with your story," I said.

"All right," he said. "Seeing you know what the purpose of Coupe Island was, you'd also know the final exercise on Coupe Island was one of the toughest ever devised."

"I'm ignorant of the details."

"Then I'll tell you what Captain Ligny and his team had to do in their final stunt," said Martin. "Or tried to do. And remember Captain Ligny as O.C. was partly responsible for the planning."

He stood up, leaned over the table and put his forefinger on the map between two ridges near the lower end of the island. This was where the dark crisscrossing lines of trench and dugout were the thickest and most complicated—and where I had lost Ligny this afternoon. Both Miss Hancock and Malcolm Blair must have heard this story before more than once, but they listened as though to a new and horrifying tale.

"It was a cold night in late November, 1941," Martin said. "Calm, black—utterly black. There was no moon and there was a heavy overcast—just the night for the climax of the training. Now, Carmichael, you mustn't imagine that Captain Ligny and his team were alone on the island. Besides the students—we can call them that—there were the usual camp personnel—cooks, batmen, ordnance men. Moreover, there were three senior officers to act as observers. Nine o'clock that night, Captain Ligny, W.O. Martin, Sergeant Giles, Sergeant Blair and the three observers went to this point. . . ."

Martin jabbed a finger toward the east end of the fourth ridge counting from the south.

"There was a bunker there the observers would stay in until the exercise was over," he said. "In the bunker, the students got their instructions for the exercise. Of course they knew the complex of trenches as well as they knew their own faces. Before they ever got to Coupe Island, they had been trained and drilled in the layout of the island—you saw evidence of that at Mount Worriong—and after they arrived here, they studied the trenches, walked through them, ran through them, crawled through them, both day and night until they could find their way blindfolded. And I do mean blindfolded.

"But the students would not know what traps were laid for them until they read their instructions—though only what traps, not where. They were each given a typewritten foolscap page and they were allowed five minutes of study under torchlight and then the instructions were taken from them. Then each was issued two items of equipment—a torch and a kind of water pistol. . . ."

Martin paused to light a cigarette. The click of his lighter had the sound of the bolt of a loaded rifle shot home.

"I have read copies of those instructions," he said. "Each was different, yet all very similar. Each student was told where he had to enter the complex, the course he had to follow and where he had to emerge. On the way, though not in this order, he would encounter grenades, land mines, flamethrowers, rifles and machine guns, all primed or loaded and adjusted to spring into action at a careless touch, though so arranged that the careless student, while getting a devil of a fright, would not be hurt. Remember that little point, Carmichael," Martin said, looking at me.

"I won't forget."

"It's important," said Martin. He drew feverishly on his cigarette. "Now the torches," he said. "Each torch beamed a different colored light. Captain Ligny's was red. My brother's was green. Blair's father's was blue and Wilfrid Giles's was orange. The torches had a double purpose. At various points in the course, each student had to flash his torch so that the observers could gauge his progress, and he also had to signal the completion of his course; three long flashes was the signal he had finished. The other purpose was, if he happened to set a weapon going, he had to flash his torch to identify himself as the culprit. Bad marks against him in that case."

Miss Hancock broke her long silence.

"Excuse me, Mr. Martin," she said, "but there's a puzzling point here I've never been able to understand. You didn't explain it before, but what was there to stop the men from flashing their torches to guide themselves through the trenches?"

"The observers in the bunker would have then seen the colored light—any kind of light in that black night," Martin said. "And there's another thing, the question of the water pistols. They were charged with liquid dye—each the same color as the respective torches. For instance, if your torch was orange, then the dye in your pistol was orange, too. This was a war game. Each student had to regard the other three as enemies. Each route had been planned to intersect all the other routes. The students weren't told this, but they *were* told if they spotted an 'enemy' they had to squirt liquid dye at him. After the exercise, any patch of dye was a good score for the marksman and a bad minus for the victim. So the students couldn't afford to show a light except as specified in the instructions."

Martin crushed out his cigarette.

"An interesting game," he said. "A dangerous game, but still a game—if there had been no Captain Ligny. In the bunker, students and observers synchronized their watches; then the students went out into the night, one by one at intervals of a minute, to take up their starting points around the field of operations. Captain Ligny"—Martin again referred to the map—"was at the northeast corner, Wilfrid Giles at the southeast, Garrett Blair at the southwest and Hugh Martin at the northwest. Each had to work into the center, then veer to the left, so that they came out of the trenches about halfway along the sides of the complex, and none of them knew where the others had been stationed—or was supposed *not* to know."

Martin turned to me.

"Before I go on, Carmichael," he said, "you must remember a very significant part of the test. The students had to delouse or deactivate every weapon they found in their path. Afterwards the observers would examine the weapons to see if the job was done. You understand, Carmichael?"

I nodded. Martin released a gusty sigh.

"They started in at 2145 hours," he said. "And you can imagine what it was like creeping through the pitch-black trenches, all the time feeling for the trip line or loose rock that would explode a land mine or have a flamethrower spouting over your head. According to the observers' subsequent reports, nothing happened until 2154, when a machine gun opened up, and there was the first of the confused accounts coming out of that terrible night. A torch flashed after the machine gun went quiet. Two of the observers said it was orange—Wilfrid Giles's torch. But the third observer said it was red—Captain Ligny's. If it was orange, Wilfrid Giles must have been well out of his course. The confusion was never settled because afterwards neither Captain Ligny nor Wilfrid Giles could clarify the question: Giles was dead and Captain Ligny too badly injured and he couldn't remember.

"Five minutes of silence, then sudden uproar—a rifle firing, a land mine exploding, a flamethrower erupting, and the flames whipped over the trenches so that the observers had a quick glimpse of the field in the lurid light. This time, there was no confusion—an orange torch shone for the rifle, a blue for the land mine, a green for the flamethrower. Giles, Blair, Martin respectively.

"At 2209 the students flashed their positions. The observers saw that the students had accomplished a little less than half of the journey. They were fairly close together; two of them—Captain Ligny and Wilfrid Giles—so near to each other they could have been in adjoining trenches or even in the same trench.

"That was the last time the students signaled their whereabouts. At 2217 all hell broke loose. A flamethrower burst into action and it did not stop as it should have. Moreover, instead of confining its fire to a safe zone, it swirled around enfilading trenches, traverses and dugouts. The heat started other weapons—more flamethrowers, machine guns, rifles, hand grenades, land mines.

"It was, as the observers reported later, like a battle constricted into a small space. The observers ran down to the trenches and went in. The flamethrowers had burned out, but the heat was intense and the smoke was thick and there was still a spasmodic banging of rifles. They all had torches, but they had to feel their way in the smoke. Near the middle of the complex, they found a body and then another, both shockingly burned. The metal 'discs identity' on the bodies identified them as Hugh Martin and Garrett Blair.

"Continuing the search, they heard someone groaning and they discovered one man stooped over another man, trying to pull him along—Captain Ligny, his face one big blister, alive; Wilfrid Giles dead, almost incinerated."

Martin paused. He looked at Malcolm Blair and Miss Hancock and me in turn. I saw his eyes were bloodshot as though he had stared into one of the exploding flamethrowers.

"At the subsequent Military Board of Inquiry," he said, "one of the aims was to determine whether Captain Ligny and the observers should be charged before a court-martial. Captain Ligny did not have much to say at the inquiry. He was still recovering from his injuries and his throat was so badly affected he could talk only with difficulty. Besides, he had only slight recollection of what occurred that night on Coupe Island. In the end, the Board exonerated the observers and recommended Captain Ligny for some recognition of his gallantry and so he got the George Cross. But I've read all the reports presented at the Inquiry, and I've studied all the maps and plans the observers prepared, and now I can make three categorical statements.

"One: The flamethrower that broke loose and spurted its fire all around had been sabotaged. Two: That flamethrower was marked on the route Captain Ligny was planned to take. Three: According to the observers' calculations, Captain Ligny was near the flamethrower when it started.

"I'll add a fourth categorical statement: If Miss Hancock's diary and the uncensored letters written by my brother and Garrett Blair had been presented to the Board of Inquiry, Captain Ligny wouldn't have had the George Cross pinned on his breast but a hangman's rope draped around his neck. Capital punishment was still in vogue twenty-eight years ago. And what have you got to say now, Carmichael?"

My mouth was so dry I had to make a strenuous effort to speak.

I said, "Your argument falls down on a vital point. Ligny must have been right in the line of fire himself. No murderer kills himself too."

"Arrgh!" said Martin. "He slipped at a crucial moment. Or he might have thought he couldn't afford to escape unharmed himself. It doesn't matter. He is a triple murderer, and we people—Miss Hancock and Blair and I—believe in the principle of a man paying for his actions."

I looked at Miss Hancock and Blair and detected no sign of dissent.

"You mean to kill him?" I said.

"Don't be so impossibly stupid," Martin said. "Our purpose is merely to point out to Ligny the appropriate action. Which brings us to the matter of *you*."

"Me?"

"Yes, and the question of your cooperation and your continued well-being. I did promise to ventilate this subject, if you remember."

Conscious of the sudden stillness of Miss Hancock and Blair, I eyed Martin and waited.

"I want to find out how far you are prepared to cooperate," he went on. "As I have already implied, I spoke to your brother-in-law last Saturday. I gathered he was satisfied—mistakenly, as is now apparent—by your attitude, but he failed to clarify one item. The *third* prize of your ill-starred expedition to Mick's Hollow the previous day. What was the third prize, Carmichael?"

My heart bumped and I felt hot blood roaring in my ears, but I produced the birthday card and flung it down on the map. Martin picked it up and as my brother-in-law had done, he read the inscription aloud.

" 'To Uncle Mick, from your loving grandnephew, Wesley. From one misfit to another.' " Martin glanced at Miss Hancock. "This would appear to relate to members of your family, Miss Hancock."

She bent her head. After some more study of the card, Martin dropped it on the table.

"Ah, well," he said, "it had no relevance to Captain Ligny, so I think we can ignore it. And also ignore Carmichael's prying into personal affairs." He looked at me. "Now for the crux of the matter, Carmichael. Where—is—Captain—Ligny?"

"I don't know," I said. "I only wish I did."

"Be careful, Carmichael. You saw Ligny this afternoon. You met him and spoke to him. Where is he hidden?"

"I did see him, but I did not speak to him. I didn't get the opportunity to speak to him."

"I'm giving you another chance," Martin growled

"I'm not a liar," I said. "And you can go to hell."

11

I climbed the steps into a world of wet bracken, pale moonlight and gathering mist. In the hut I switched on the battery lamp, but the place was so forlorn and chilly that I located my torch and went outside to search for kindling. Finding heaps of dry dead bracken fronds against the walls sheltered by the eaves, I carried a big bundle of them inside, set them burning in the fireplace and built a hollow cairn of briquettes over the flames.

I knelt on the hearth and huffed and puffed until the briquettes caught a light. The fire established, I set about getting my house in order—my rations stacked along the wall opposite the fire; the Primus stove and kerosene and methylated spirits nearby; the pup tent lying flat in the middle of the floor; on top of the tent the inflated mattress; on top of the mattress the sleeping bag. Next I filled two cooking pots with spring water against the needs of the morning, stoked up the fire, and then in front of it I sat in the chair that Blair had left behind, dusted my shin with sulpha powder and began to think about Ligny.

I wondered where he was now, wondered whether he was skulking in some heat-blistered hole in what Martin had termed the field of operations, shivering in fear of retribution or anguishing with remorse. The great unconformity. It would appear as if the great unconformity had existed in my imagination. At that, I rebelled. I still had my belief in the Lewis Ligny I had known, the man who had created his little lake and had displayed ingenuous pleasure over his ships and railroads.

But where to find him, and if I could find him, would he listen to me? He had turned me down at Festival Hall and he had run away from me this afternoon.

I should have been looking for him at this very moment. But I ached with fatigue and my brain was clogged, and so I drank a shot of whiskey, stripped off to my underclothes and crept into the sleeping bag. I was asleep before I could take five deep breaths.

In the dream I was deep in a bunker overwhelmed in the blaze of a flamethrower, fighting the panic that paralyzed my body, and there was someone near me yelling and thumping an alarm. I broke free from the paralysis and opened my eyes, and the only conflagration I saw was in the dying embers in the fireplace. But the voice still called and the thumping continued. I switched on the lamp.

"Who's there?"

"Miss Hancock," the voice said.

I rolled out of the sleeping bag, pulled on my trousers, whipped into a jersey and padded barefooted over the cold floor. I opened the door and it *was* Miss Hancock. She stood in the pallid moonlight, hazy in the drifting ground mist, her furry hat beaded with moisture and her high boots damp from walking through the bracken.

"Mr. Carmichael, I'm sorry," she said, her eyes black shadows in her white face. "It's two o'clock in the morning, but I must talk to you."

"Of course, Miss Hancock."

She entered and I shifted the chair nearer to the hearth and I sat her in it. She held out gloved hands to the feeble fire.

"You're cold," I said. "Excuse me for a moment."

I pulled on socks and boots, donned my duffle coat, picked up the torch and hurried outside for a fresh supply of dead fronds. Back again in the hut, I dropped the fronds on the fire and when the flames leapt, added more briquettes to the blaze. Then I studied Miss Hancock's wan countenance.

"I've got some whiskey," I said. "Would you like some?"

"I'd like a hot drink, if you please."

"Hot chocolate?"

"I'd love it," she said. "You're so kind, Mr. Carmichael."

"A pleasure," I said mechanically, and I went to the other end of the hut, lifted the Primus stove and carried it to the hearth.

"Please, not the Primus," Miss Hancock said. "The noise, Mr. Carmichael. I prefer silence. If anything happens outside, I want to hear it."

So something had really gone wrong. I balanced a pot of water on two burning briquettes and harried the fire until the water was simmering. But now I too was listening to the mist-filled silence enveloping the hut.

I poured hot chocolate into two mugs, gave one to Miss Hancock and, with the other warming my hands, leaned against the mantelpiece and regarded Miss Hancock. A stately old lady, yet fragile and frightened.

"What's the trouble, Miss Hancock?"

She sipped her chocolate.

"Lovely," she said. She raised her dark eyes to me. "I've made a discovery about myself. I've always thought that loneliness was a privilege. Much of my life has been lonely and I never complained. But I couldn't bear to be alone on the yacht tonight and so, Mr. Carmichael, I've foisted myself on you."

"You were alone?"

137

"I woke up an hour ago," she said, "hearing stealthy noises on the yacht. They lasted for a minute; then they ceased and there was only the rippling of water. And the creaking of timber like a groan, and that made the silence all the worse. I got up and looked through the yacht and I found I was alone. Mr. Blair and Mr. Martin had gone. How or why I don't know, but I—I confess I became panicky and so—please forgive me, Mr. Carmichael—I'm here."

She drank more chocolate.

"I'm glad you thought of me," I said. "And now what do we think about Martin and Blair?"

"One of two things," Miss Hancock said. "Although my nerves played up with me, I could still reason. Either they discovered Captain Ligny stealing aboard the yacht and they have gone in pursuit of him, or they have gone searching for him, unencumbered by you or me. Which idea would you pick, Mr. Carmichael?"

"The second."

Miss Hancock sighed.

"I'm afraid you're right," she said. "Now I want you to understand I'm entirely with Mr. Martin and Mr. Blair in their attitude to Captain Ligny. I'm an old woman and I can't permit—if it's in my power—a horrible crime to go unpunished. When I think of Wilfrid Giles and Hugh Martin and Garrett Blair, I must have their pain expiated. Evil has to be rebuked or all I believe in is worthless. But I can't agree to this stealing through the night and creeping on a man unawares. I'm afraid that Mr. Martin and Mr. Blair could be responsible for something just as horrible as Captain Ligny's crime. What can we do about it, Mr. Carmichael?"

I looked at my watch. The time was two thirty-five. If Miss Hancock's estimation was right, Martin and Blair had a start of more than an hour and a half. There had been time for them to reach the fused granite and bracken-choked complex at the other end of the island, time to get their hands on Ligny—

"There's only one thing to do," I said. "Stop them, or try to."

"Good," said Miss Hancock. She stood up, drank the rest of her chocolate and put her mug on the mantelpiece. "We'll start straightaway."

"*You're* not going," I said.

"Of course I'm going, Mr. Carmichael."

"But it's unthinkable, Miss Hancock. At this time of night, on rugged ground and the bracken sopping wet? Oh, no, Miss Hancock. You stay here warm and safe beside the fire."

Miss Hancock raised her chin in her most dignified manner.

"I did not run from a lonely yacht to stay alone in a lonely hut," she said. "You think I'm old and feeble and you can see yourself finishing up having to carry me. You won't have to carry me. I was nervy when I found Mr. Martin and Mr. Blair gone, but I'm tough. I'm a throwback to the old Hancocks who lived to a hundred. If you go, I go. If I stay, you stay. So lead on, Mr. Carmichael, like King Wenceslaus. I'll be right in your footsteps. . . ."

In the last hour, the ground mist had fattened into a fog that rolled in from the southeast in dark capricious waves of gloom. One minute the torch revealed a stretch of dark wet bracken; the next it illumined a gray opaque wall and, as though in funereal step, the moon slowly weaved in and out of the murk.

At first I was very conscious of Miss Hancock behind me. I had brought my flask of whiskey (as well as two slabs of chocolate) and wondering when I would have to apply the whiskey to a collapsing female, I often flashed the torch back and looked at Miss Hancock's face above the scarf I had made her wrap around her throat. Though she rarely spoke, she never failed to smile and her step never faltered, and so my worry about her gradually lessened.

The indomitable Miss Hancock. But there was no need to tempt Providence. On the fifth ridge we came to, the torch shone into an old dugout and I found a comparatively dry spot on the parapet step.

"Time for a spell, Miss Hancock," I said.

With the torch probing into the fog-smothered swale ahead, we sat in companionable silence until Miss Hancock asked where we were now.

"More than a mile from the hut," I replied. "Right in front of us is a hollow about two hundred yards wide. Perhaps three hundred. If I remember rightly, there are a lot of trenches broken in and overgrown with bracken, so we'll have to go carefully. But over the next ridge there's a great deal more and there'll be barbed wire too. The field of operations, as Martin called it."

"The place where we have to look for Mr. Martin and Mr. Blair?"

"And Lewis Ligny, too, perhaps."

"I notice," she said, "you never refer to him as *Captain* Ligny."

"I never knew a Captain Ligny, Miss Hancock. I only know a good friend called Lewis Ligny."

"You're loyal," she said. "And I have no doubt it was your loyalty that took you to Mick's Hollow, where you found your sister— There's no need for surprise, Mr. Carmichael. Your sister went there with my concurrence and that would have gone for you, too, for I did offer to take you there myself. But why, Mr. Carmichael, did you take the birthday card?"

"Mere curiosity," I said, and I wished I could see her face. I could not dare to lift the torch at her. "I knew it had nothing to do with Ligny and I should have left it where I found it. But I was inquisitive."

"I had never heard of it until you showed it to Mr. Martin tonight," she said. "But it has a bitter truth about the Hancocks. 'To one misfit from another.' The time and place for confession—eh, Mr. Carmichael?—a lonely fogbound island in the middle of the night. *All* Hancocks were misfits and

140

they were hard on people who hurt them, but a thousandfold harder when the offender happened to be a Hancock. Uncle Mick quarreled with his father and exiled himself to his hut. Wesley's quarrel was even more bitter. Unforgivable things were said on both sides and he was permanently deleted from the family."

"I'm sorry I ever saw the card," I said.

"Don't be sorry. If you hadn't found it, I wouldn't have it now."

"Now?"

"You forgot to take it when Mr. Martin was finished with it, so I confiscated it for myself—for the record, as it were."

To store among the relics of one deleted from the family, I reflected. But were there any relics of Wesley Hancock back at Worriong Cottage? I hadn't seen there even a snap of the wayward Wesley.

Venturing greatly, I said, "What kind of fellow was your nephew really?"

Miss Hancock drew in a sharp breath and I thought, Carmichael, now for a kick in the pants, and how! I was lucky. After a pause she began to speak of Wesley, building up a picture of the kind of man a small boy, who scribbled his name over portraits, would become. As she talked, it gradually soaked into me that Wesley must have been much the same type as the four soldiers she depicted in her diary—big, tough, game, reckless. *And* hotheaded.

Then another thought arose—not slowly, but fast and hard. She was lamenting her lost nephew and was requiting the family's treatment of him by trying to right the wrong done to Wilfrid Giles. To contend for two of Captain Ligny's victims were Martin and Baird, but as she herself had said, she was here to stand up for Giles. A form of sublimation. Both Wilfrid and Wesley were dead. In avenging the one, she was doing penance for the other.

Presently she fell silent, then she said, "So much for Wesley Hancock. I suggest we push on, Mr. Carmichael."

141

She stood up and I stood up too, and then she was clutching at me, for a dull explosion broke the hush of the fog.

"A gunshot!" Miss Hancock said.

That bloody Martin! Then I recollected the hollow sound of the explosion and the ever so slight tremor my feet had felt in the ground.

"No gunshot," I said, "but some kind of charge fired underground."

"I'm afraid," Miss Hancock said. "Do let's hurry."

She had no thought of abandoning the chase, but she didn't withdraw her hand from my elbow, and so we went down into the fog of the swale, Miss Hancock clinging to my arm. I didn't object. I was scared myself and I was grateful for not being alone.

We breasted the sixth ridge, Miss Hancock's breath misting quickly in the cold air. On the crest a fissure opened in the fog, and moonlight revealed a tangle of ancient trenches and interlinking traverses shadowy in the bracken. Straight ahead I made out the bare scorched granite where I had lost Ligny's tracks, but when I glanced to the left, I failed to distinguish any hump or mound that could have been the bunker from which the three observers had watched.

Another sluggish bank of fog poured diagonally into the swale. Just as it absorbed the scorched granite, there was a faint swift yellow glow attended simultaneously by a second boom that shook the ground. And then Miss Hancock and I could see only fog.

We went down into the fog slowly, fearfully. In the eerie chilly murk, we couldn't do otherwise, for the torch beam reached no more than a pace ahead of our feet. We edged along parapets, felt our way around dugouts and when it appeared there was no other way, I lifted Miss Hancock over wet, bracken-filled ditches.

At length we arrived on a plat of level ground and we paused to get our bearings. I felt a light pressure of air on my left cheek and I beamed the torch up into an oblique spectral movement of the fog passing over my right shoulder. So we were still heading in the direction of the scorched granite.

"Are you all right, Miss Hancock?" I asked.

"When I'm not, I'll tell you," she said.

We continued for ten or eleven slow paces, and then Miss Hancock stopped and tugged my arm.

"What's the matter—"

"Sh-h!" she whispered. "Put the light out. We have company."

I eased back the torch button. Miss Hancock felt for my hand and pointed it to left.

"There," she said so softly I sensed rather than heard her whisper.

There was only blackness pressing wetly into our faces. I saw nothing, heard nothing—I did hear something, a small tapping noise right by my side, and my skin tautened icily. And then I understood—drops of water were falling from my duffle coat onto the bracken.

"Listen," said Miss Hancock under her breath.

"Only water—"

"No, no. Can't you hear it?" Miss Hancock stood stiffly for thirty seconds. "He's gone," she said. "Or it is gone." And she sighed.

"I didn't hear a thing except—"

"I know—water dripping." Miss Hancock spoke more in her normal tone. "I have always had abnormally acute hearing. But he's gone—I can assure you of that. I suggest we look for whatever he was up to."

I thumbed the torch alight and we advanced cautiously through the bracken. I mightn't have had the quality of Miss Hancock's ears, but my nose was keen enough and I detected a familiar odor. Faint at first, but growing with every forward step until, when the torch shone into a dugout strewn with fresh earth and riven rock, the full acrid flavor stung my nostrils.

"Dynamite," I said to Miss Hancock, who was wrinkling her nose. "And not long fired. We saw it and heard it too."

"There were two explosions."

"Both fired by the same hand, Miss Hancock."

"Mr. Martin and Mr. Blair or Captain Ligny?" she asked, and proceeded to answer the question herself. "Captain Ligny, of course. I heard only one man running away."

"I'm afraid so, though I couldn't testify to the running."

"Well, he did run," said Miss Hancock. "But why blow up a dugout?"

"I can try and find out." I turned the torch on Miss Hancock. "I'm going to crawl into the dugout. Will you be all right in the dark?"

"Can't I come, too?"

"No, you can't, Miss Hancock. Will you promise me you won't move from this spot until I get back?"

She promised, although reluctantly, and I dropped down onto the rubble and beamed the torch around. The dugout had been hollowed out in shale under a shelf of granite and the opening was blocked with torn rock almost up to the overhang. Seeing what I had to do, I emptied my pockets of pipe, whiskey and chocolate and placed them on the bank. I put the torch down, dragged the larger boulders out of the way and then picking up the torch again, I crawled sidelong fashion under the overhang. I wriggled onto my stomach and swung the torch around.

I could see only the fallen rock and the jagged shale at the back and the granite above my head, looking as if it were about to plunge down and crush me. The smell of exploded nitroglycerine was very strong in here.

I took a final glance around—and the light shone dully on a rusted object that was *not* stone, almost entirely buried in the rubble down in the right-hand corner. I had to get it, of course, and I slithered down to it, ignoring the rocks until a dart of agony halted me. My sore shin had taken a fresh assault, but the rusty object was now in reach of my fingers.

I crawled out from under the overhang, limped over to where Miss Hancock was waiting patiently and displayed my prize.

"A cashbox!" she said. "Anything in it, Mr. Carmichael?"

I shook the box and Miss Hancock listened to the sound of soggy rustling.

"We'll soon find out what it is, Miss Hancock." I cast the torch beam around and saw a lump of rock that could be used for a seat. "We might as well sit comfortably—or as comfortably as we can."

Miss Hancock took the torch and the tin box and I lifted her safely from the bank and we seated ourselves.

I said, "Will you hold the torch please, Miss Hancock?"

The rusted buckled lid resisted my fingers, but my clasp knife was successful and the lid grated open. There were two items in the box, both creased by time and gray with mildew. One was a half sheet of paper folded once, the other a sealed envelope.

I lifted the half sheet out carefully and gingerly unfolded it. In the beam of the torch were three lines of hasty handwriting and, despite the ravages of moisture, the words were legible.

Will the finder please deliver the accompanying letter to the lady whose name and address appear on the envelope?

Underneath was the scrawled signature:

Wilfrid Giles

I did not have to lift out the envelope to see what name the letter bore. The superscription looked up at us from the box.

Miss Rhoda Hancock
"Worriong Cottage"
Mount Worriong, Vic.

12

There was a pause, then Miss Hancock spoke calmly.

"As the song says, I have not brought my specs with me. Please read the writing to me, Mr. Carmichael."

I complied, and she said, "So my eyes were not mistaken. Oh, dear! Well, will the finder discharge Wilfrid Giles's request? We might as well get it over quickly."

She touched my hand and I felt the tremor of her fingers through her glove. I took out the clasp knife again and cut the seal of the envelope to find that the letter had become stuck to the flap. I eased the blade through the gum and delicately withdrew and unfolded three sheets that were as pulpy as damp blotting-paper.

Miss Hancock moved the torch closer and I read aloud everything I saw.

> Coupe Island
> 11 P.M., 5/11/41

Dear Miss Hancock,

Or should I say, Dear Aunt Rhoda? You didn't object that evening of the dinner party at Worriong Cottage.

If and when you get this letter, you will know I am dead, and very likely Hugh Martin and Garrett Blair as well. I ought to be writing to Elspeth too, but I'm not game. I can't face up to talk to Elspeth about murder—*my* murder, but I know you, Aunt Rhoda. You're not the fainting kind. You will know what to do about Captain Ligny.

Tomorrow night, the four of us go out on our final test on Coupe Island. After that, the official directive is we will be posted to some forward area in the Pacific to wait for the Japs. The heads tell us it is a matter of weeks, even days, before the Japs come into the war, and we'll have plenty of scope for our peculiar talents.

Captain Ligny might see something of the Japs, but we, Hugh, Garrett and I, won't. Captain Ligny will see to that, especially in my case. I won't go into the details of Captain Ligny's treatment of us. There isn't enough time, and, anyway, you have already learned something about him. But tomorrow night there will be accidental fatalities—we are as sure as death of that.

For me, surer. Captain Ligny has always hated me. You and Elspeth saw evidence of that in Mick's Hollow, and two nights ago he got me on my own and said, "Giles, if anything happens to you, don't worry, I'll see your effects are sent to anywhere you like."

So there it is, Aunt Rhoda. There will be an "accident" tomorrow and now you know what to do.

We don't know the details of the test, but we have a general idea of the official procedure, so I've pinched a small tin cashbox from the Orderly Office. I'll put this letter in the box and hide it somewhere near where I have to start the course. There will be three officers to observe the test. If there's an accident, they'll go over the course with a fine-tooth comb and they'll find the box and the letter.

My love to Elspeth and to you, Aunt Rhoda.

Yours,

Wilfrid Giles

P.S. I've just thought of something. I'll tell Captain Ligny I'm leaving evidence against him in case of anything happening. So, perhaps, there will be no "accident."

We sat for a while, cold and silent. Only wisps of fog moved, sifting through the torch's bright cone of light like the melancholy thoughts that sifted through my mind. Judg-

147

ing by Miss Hancock's shadowy face, her reflections were no less somber.

"I think I wouldn't now refuse some of your whiskey, Mr. Carmichael," she said at last. "And a bite of that emergency chocolate to hide the whiskey's taste."

We each drank a dram, sharing the screw-on jigger that stoppered the flask, and then we chewed bits of chocolate.

"So now we know why he blew up the dugout," Miss Hancock said. "He had to try to get rid of the last damning shred of evidence."

I had nothing to say to that and Miss Hancock gave me a long look.

"Don't feel so badly," she said. "You'll get over it."

"What about *you,* Miss Hancock?" I said. "It's twenty-eight years now, but you haven't forgotten."

"Not the same thing," Miss Hancock said. "Captain Ligny never disillusioned me. You have been betrayed, but you'll get over it." She withdrew into her memories for a minute. Then she continued: "It's peculiar, now the time is on us for the reckoning with Captain Ligny, I don't feel it's all that important. Peculiar, after keeping my diaries and poring over them for twenty-eight years. I want to face him to see if he does understand what he really did—"

She stopped and gazed into the darkness of the fog.

"No," she said. "I don't even want to do that. All I want is to get back home, burn my diaries, start digging in the garden again and read my books and watch the sun rise over the mount. I don't want to see Captain Ligny."

Her reference to her books evoked a pertinent question, the matter of Thoreau's *Walden,* the book that had landed us, Miss Hancock and me, on Coupe Island. I did not voice the question, but it seemed Miss Hancock was thinking somewhat on the same lines.

"It's very fitting, I think," she said, "that you, the one to return my Thoreau to me, should also be the finder of the letter from Wilfrid. Altogether symmetrical. But"—her mind swerved away from mine—"there's no need for you to do any more. You don't have to *see* Captain Ligny."

I could have agreed unreservedly with Miss Hancock except for two words she herself had used. "Altogether symmetrical" was Miss Hancock's phrase. There was an element running through Wilfrid Giles's letter that was *not* symmetrical; in fact, it was right out of shape. If Giles had to write a letter, why not write to the observers on the spot? Better still, face the observers and make his accusations in person?

Then there was the dissonant note in the postscript.

I'll tell Captain Ligny I'm leaving evidence against him in case of anything happening.

Wilfrid Giles must have fulfilled his intention, otherwise Ligny, twenty-eight years afterward, wouldn't have gone around blowing up old dugouts. But that wasn't the jarring note the postscript struck. I was still trying to work out where the discord lay when Miss Hancock gave an exclamation.

"Look up, Mr. Carmichael!"

More solace, I told myself, but that wasn't it at all. There was something to see and something to hear as well. A cold southeast breeze came rustling through the bracken and started the fog swirling off to the northwest. Gathering force, the wind tore gaps in the murk and a few solitary stars appeared overhead. A great stretch of the Milky Way followed. The moon sailed out, silvering the retreating banks of fog and striking little white sparks from the black sea, and the waves raised their voice in beating against the island.

Miss Hancock and I could see each other now in the moonlight and I switched out the torch. Then I flicked it on again and began flashing the light.

"Why?" asked Miss Hancock.

I showed her the two torches zigzagging across the swale; then I helped her out of the dugout.

I was sure of trouble as soon as I saw their faces, Martin's

149

black with anger and suspicion, Blair's as though he were in the ring up against a dirty fighter. However, they held their animosity in check while we exchanged explanations. On their part, they said they had suspected that Captain Ligny could have been lurking in or around the fiord and they had gone to search for him, but the fog defeated them and they had returned to the yacht only to discover Miss Hancock had disappeared. They had then repaired to my hut and I was also missing, and consequently they had been looking for us the rest of the night.

"You don't take much notice of warnings, Carmichael," said Martin, ire thrumming deep in his voice.

In reply I said Miss Hancock did not like being deserted on the yacht ("It was damned thoughtless of you, leaving her alone") and so she had come to me for help and advice. As for our going out into the fog, there was a very good reason.

"You gave the reason yourself," I said to Martin. "You stated your purpose was to point out to Ligny the appropriate way out. Miss Hancock and I could only conclude that you and Blair knew where you could find Ligny and stand over him till he took the appropriate action. Make him kill himself, Martin. Make him jump over a cliff or put a bullet in himself—that's what you mean."

Martin swore under his breath and Blair took a step forward and aligned himself at Martin's side. They were nearly at the boiling point—very nearly. The wind blew over the bracken and the moldering mounds in the hollow.

"A new development has arisen," said Miss Hancock, trying to avert the storm. "The letter Wilfrid Giles wrote to me."

I thought that Miss Hancock had made a bad mistake, that she had precipitated the crisis she wanted to avoid, but it became clear very soon that, no matter what Miss Hancock did or did not do, Martin was bent on settling my hash.

When Miss Hancock produced the letter I had found in the dugout, Martin and Blair bent over it with their torches blazing.

"So you found it as a result of Captain Ligny blowing up the dugout," said Martin.

"Yes," said Miss Hancock.

"Wonderful!" said Martin. "Now I'm just waiting to shove this into Captain Ligny's face. I just want to see his face—his dirty murdering face."

"I want to see his face, too," I said.

Both Martin and Blair looked up from the letter.

"*You* won't see him," Martin said.

"What do you mean?"

"I'm sick and tired of you, Carmichael. No more running loose for you. You're going to be locked up as soon as we get back to the boat. And if you won't go quietly, we'll drag you there."

In some circumstances, you should never let the other fellow know what you propose to do. According to the postscript, Wilfrid Giles must have made that mistake. I jumped at Martin, shouldered him into Blair, shoved both down into the dugout and raced up the ridge beyond the scorched granite, praying desperately there were no holes to fall into, no barbed wire to hook around my legs.

I gained the crest and took the force of the wind in my face. Angry shouts behind me spurred me on and I went charging down the slope through the wet bracken. Five paces, ten, fifteen, twenty, I counted to myself; twenty-five, thirty, thirty-five, forty—then I dropped flat in the bracken just as two torches flashed over the ridge. The torches, swiveling from side to side, revealed merely the tossing bracken, and Martin and Blair ran past me.

I waited until they were a hundred yards away, then I nipped back the way I had come, coasted over the ridge and came face to face with Miss Hancock.

"I thought you'd be back," she said. "I've got your things for you. You'll need them."

My pipe, torch, flask and the remainder of the chocolate. I stowed them in my pockets, stole back to the ridge, peered

151

over and saw the torches of Blair and Martin zigzagging to the west. So I had to go east. I returned to Miss Hancock.

"What about you, Miss Hancock?"

"I'm rather too old for running," she said. "Whether Mr. Martin and Mr. Blair will accompany me or not, I'm for the yacht. A hot bath and a warm bed for me."

"I'll take you there, Miss Hancock."

"Goodness, no. Your worry is Captain Ligny, Mr. Carmichael. Don't waste time with me."

"You're wonderful, Miss Hancock," I said.

I kissed her, had a second look at the torches still ranging to the west and started in the opposite direction. I wondered whether I had kissed Miss Hancock for putting herself tacitly on my side of the fence or because she was Miss Hancock. The latter, I decided. I had known her for a long time—nine days, at least.

I had another view of the torches half an hour later. I had arrived at a hummock above the eastern cliffs and on the lee-side I sheltered from the wind and drank a tot of whiskey. From here I saw the torches wavering slowly northward. Martin and Blair were doing the right thing by Miss Hancock—

A sudden thought struck me. One of the men was escorting Miss Hancock to the yacht while the other stayed behind to search for me. Then I gave that idea away. It was very unlikely either of them had deprived himself of light in that maze of trenches and barbed-wire entanglements.

Therefore I could depend on some respite. Watching the torches disappear behind a ridge, I took another dram of whiskey and got out my pipe. Yes, I thought, I could risk a smoke; the smell of burning tobacco would be quickly dissipated in this stiff breeze; as for the flare of a match—well, I could cover that up.

With the pipe going and the bowl warming my fingers, I leaned back in the bracken and looked at the moon. Nearly full moon, I realized. The wind whistled through the bracken, and the waves burst heavily on the rocks below. Five o'clock in the morning of Wednesday, August 27. I had been twenty-four hours on Coupe Island and I was as far away from Ligny as at Worriong Cottage. Much farther, because I had lost—yes, the vision that had taken me to Worriong Cottage.

The vision that had generated with Ligny's lake. Again I pictured the little lake, the ports and ships, the cliffs and hills and railways. After a while, the details building up more clearly in my mind, I made the discovery that so far I had concentrated on only one aspect of the lake—its shape, the Merino-like outline that linked the lake with Walden Pond and Coupe Island. But I had forgotten that in an icon every part had a significant meaning, and in this new light I reviewed the lake and its surrounds once more.

It came to me then that if one could erect a stupendous mirror around Coupe Island right against the shoreline, one would see in the reflection a reproduction, gigantically magnified, of the cliffs and ridges and hollows surrounding Ligny's lake. Conversely, if one could contrive a series of reciprocal mirrors around Ligny's lake, the final mirror would give the reflection of a miniature Coupe Island. All Ligny had done in his annex was transpose water and land and land and water.

Everything Ligny had constructed in his annex had meaning, and the assumption at once had confirmation. The secluded fiord on Coupe Island harboring Martin's hired yacht and Ligny's yawl had its counterpart in Ligny's lake. The fiord was situated in what one could call the throat of the one-legged Merino. In Ligny's model, in the same relative position, was one of the three ports that Ligny had made.

It followed logically that if I explored the sites on Coupe Island corresponding to the other ports on Ligny's lake, I would find more man-made work, more steps cut in the cliffs, more caverns, more bunkers, more evidences of the army's occupation.

One of these two ports was at the southwest corner of the lake; the other was farther up the western shores at the head

153

of an acute inlet (which would, of course, correspond on Coupe Island to an acute cape).

It should be simple to locate both sites on the island. But what could I do about the remainder of the symbols? Everything Ligny created, I thought, had a meaning. Everything? No, not the purely mechanical devices—the trains, ships, mines, conveyor belts. They were the garnish to the real significance. I could see Ligny designing his little world as a memorial to a shocking climacteric, and his delight in accomplishment was the measure of his misery. Like the sea and the land, he had transposed happiness and lamentation.

And then I comprehended where my thinking had got me. I was admitting at last that Lewis Ligny was a threefold murderer. I huddled back into the bracken just as wretched as Ligny himself. In a little while I dozed off in spite of myself.

13

When I woke up, stiff and cold and still despondent, the sun had risen, the seabirds were wheeling and calling over the cliffs, the wind blew from the northwest and a high curly net of cirrus portended a change in the weather.

I pulled myself up to my feet and stamped around to set my blood flowing. My shin was aching, but only from the cold, for the inflammation had disappeared. Good old sulpha powder! I climbed to the top of the mound and surveyed the scene—the ridges, the rolling bracken, the hillock beyond the huts, the dark blue circle of sea. No one moved—at least, in my range of sight—and no smoke rose from the fiord. I hoped Miss Hancock was sleeping peacefully. I didn't care a damn about Martin and Blair as long as they kept out of my way.

I had two sites to examine, the southwest corner and the promontory farther up the west shoreline. I ate breakfast—a lump of chocolate washed down with a mouthful of whiskey—and pursued by inquisitive gulls, I set off around the cliffs for the southwest corner. But trapped into thinking of Wilfrid Giles's letter, I swerved to the right and in two minutes

I was standing over the dugout where I had found the cash-box. The box was still there, lying on top of the rubble blown out by Ligny's dynamite, but the letter had gone and so too the smell of nitroglycerine.

The postscript, I thought.

I've just thought of something. I'll tell Captain Ligny I'm leaving evidence against him in case of anything happening. So, perhaps, there will be no "accident."

I tried to pin down the feeling of discrepancy. I looked at the scorched granite and gazed over the "field of operations," the maze of trenches and saps and parapets, all crumbling and overgrown with bracken, and I pictured the four men waiting twenty-eight years ago for zero hour. Here, where I now stood, Wilfrid Giles. Garrett Blair, three hundred yards to the west. Hugh Martin, the same distance north of Blair. Captain Ligny, on the last corner, north from Giles and east from Martin.

A cold black night, the watches ticking on to 2145 hours. Wilfrid Giles, his "evidence" just hidden, perhaps thinking in little spurts of Miss Hancock and Elspeth. Garrett Blair, thinking of his wife and son. Hugh, thinking maybe of his parents and brother. Captain Ligny, thinking of Giles's warning: "I'm leaving evidence." All four enveloped in the blackness, rendered blacker by hate. Then the watches registering nine forty-five, they slip silently into the inferno waiting for them.

Almost the discrepancy surfaced. I almost had it in my hand, as it were, open for inspection; then it was gone and all I had was an intense feeling of frustration.

With the gulls again in attendance, I cut over the ridges to the forbidding bluff where I had quenched my thirst yesterday, then headed west until I had turned the corner. Here I slowed down, picking a careful way along the brink of the cliffs, examining every upthrust rock and peering into every cleft and crevice. And I had my reward—visible evidence that man had been here before me, a ramp curling steeply around a massive concave buttress of shale capped with granite. A path, not a set of steps as in the fiord, and if a stone were dropped from the tip of the granite, it would have splashed into the sea thirty feet out from the toe of the buttress.

I could see the path for fifty feet; then it vanished around to the far side of the bulwark. I walked along the top of the cliffs for a hundred yards or more, hoping to get a view of where the path led, but all I saw was a huge bulge of rock leaning out against the sea.

I glanced up at the gulls soaring overhead, wishing I had their wings; then I returned to the path and again studied the descent. Two feet wide, the grade nearly one in one, the edge looking as if it would shatter under even a gull's tread—no, I didn't like it.

I ventured a step straight down, then drew back quickly. The gulls were mewing as though crying long odds on the poor boob finishing up in the drink. I made a second attempt, sidelong, facing the sea, then I switched around to face the cliff, not because I was scared of heights but because there were cracks in the rock to which my fingers could cling.

So I edged down precariously, the gulls seeming to voice their disappointment I was still on the path. I inched around under the overhanging granite, took a glance ahead and swore softly. The path ended dead against a solid wall of rock and there was no possible way for a gravity-anchored man to discover what was on the other side. This time, the cries of the gulls had a mocking note. If only they had liked, they could have told me what was there.

I descended to the wall, leaned back against it, looked at the arc of the sea, at the swiftly receding perspective of cliffs, and wondered why the hell the path had been made. A useless proceeding, unless it had been a wartime exercise for commandos practicing a stealthy entry into an enemy stronghold. It was possible that Ligny himself had had a hand in constructing it. At all events, he knew of the path because he had marked its position on his lake.

Poor Ligny!

The gulls condescended to watch over my progress up the path.

From a knoll on top, I could see the coast trending slightly east of north and then curving west to a bold headland. This was my next destination, the third of the "port" sites around Ligny's lake. Through the air, it would have been scarcely a mile, but for me, butting through bracken and detouring around trenches and barbed wire, it was more like two miles. Two sweating miles, and I walked with my coat slung over my shoulder.

It took me twenty-five minutes to reach the trunk of the cape. From then on, it was a matter of scrambling out to the headland between narrow converging lines of cliffs. To the right, the coast bent back north and east to the tiny strip of beach where Amos Waller had landed me yesterday, and I could see over my right shoulder the hillock and the lonely huts below it.

I halted two hundred yards from the headland. Here the cape was less than eighty yards wide and, on either side, I saw a breach in the rock that was obviously the start of a pathway down the cliffs. Once more, Ligny's lake had been proved authentic.

Choosing the left-hand notch, I descended an easy four-foot ledge, still escorted by gulls. As I neared the water's edge, I saw that the path had ducked into a gloomy vaulted recess, circled out and up and away through a man-hewn cutting, presumably to go on to the right-hand notch. But there was nothing to remark except the rock and the water flooding into the recess. I took my torch out and flashed its beam over cracks and clefts and groined arches. There was no secret cave, no stealthy tunnel, no sign of Ligny.

I went around to the cutting and sat down. I surveyed the

quadrant of sea in front of me; then again I peered into the recess. I remembered Mr. Gemmell's remark it was Coupe Island where he had got the itch for yachting. Here, very likely, was the place he had taken his first lessons in managing small vessels.

A pretty theory, Carmichael, but it doesn't point the way to Ligny. I took out the flask, drank the little whiskey that remained and shoved the flask back into my coat pocket. Then I became aware of a murmur that had no relation to the mewing of gulls. The murmur rose into an unmistakable vibrating throb. I jumped up and peeped over the slab of rock on the seaward side and there was the *Erica* curling in from the north and heading straight for the cave.

There was a brief turmoil at the stern as the screws went into reverse; then the diesels died and the yacht drifted bow on to me scarcely sixty yards away. Martin and Blair were on the sheltered bridge, but I couldn't see Miss Hancock. Suddenly the searchlight above the bridge burned and I dived down behind the rock to watch the dazzling beam highlight every node and crook and dimple in the cave.

The light winked out and the diesels went into action. I ventured a glance over the slab. The *Erica* backed away from the headland; then with a surge of power she wheeled and went creaming away to the south at a good twelve knots.

They had not seen me. They were not even looking for me. And with that came the tardy perception that Martin knew everything I knew about Coupe Island. Much more, in fact. My knowledge was the outcome of intuition and lucky guessing, but Martin's was based on the hard facts of army records. Therefore it was inevitable the *Erica*'s next port of call was the southwest corner.

Now I did damn my beef-headed thinking. Here, at the headland, as Ligny's lake had indicated, was this path clearly defined and easily accessible. At the fiord, likewise indicated by Ligny's lake, were the hewn steps leading down to the little haven. Then, at the southwest corner, there must also be a practicable track, else Ligny's lake was foolishness.

I started up the path like a scared rabbit. Beyond the cutting the slope became a broad mild ramp like the one I had descended and I pelted up until I came out onto the spine of the headland. I took a glance at the *Erica* scudding south and though I was already desperately blown, I plunged ahead into a hard run.

When I had reached the main body of the island, the yacht was almost at her destination. I saw her slacken speed and she wheeled sharply to port and drove slowly toward the cliffs and vanished. I ran, trying to forget the deadweight of my legs and the fire in my lungs. I want time, I thought, time to get there before the yacht could reappear and sail away with Ligny, leaving me alone on the island. That, surely, would be the acme of Martin's triumph.

By the grace of heaven, I found the track. Two hundred yards north of the first abortive ramp, I saw a gap in the bracken fringing a shelf jutting out at right angles from the cliff. Impossible to detect by someone heading north unless he knew of its existence, it was plainly visible *from* the north, and I looked down a wide path that curved to the left around a gigantic bulge of rock. I went down the path, dragging in gulps of air. I was aware of the rock on my left side, of the sea on the right; aware too that the early net of cirrus had thickened into an ashen porridge spread and the wind now blew spitefully directly from the west.

I gathered my coat under my arm and paid heed to the path coming into view around the bulge of rock. The slope steepened and I arrived at the beginning of foot-high steps, but I could not see where the path led until I saw a scissure in the rock above me. The scissure widened into a chasm and the chasm filled out into a great cavern. It would have been a cathedral of Egyptian gloom but for the lights of the *Erica*, tethered to a stone landing, her gangway lifting and falling to the swell, her fenders chafing at the rock.

Peering beyond the yacht, I made out the inner rampart

160

cave and tunnel openings and recessed cubicles well above the waterline. Enough space to accommodate a platoon of Lignys. But it was quiet despite the wind and the waves. I started down the last steps to the landing. Too quiet, too ominous. Martin emerged from behind a hump of rock and he had a pistol aimed at my chest.

"On board, Carmichael," he said. "This time there'll be no shoving me out of the way."

On the yacht, Malcolm Blair appeared from the midships companion to expedite my capture.

Ligny was in the main saloon, tied hand and foot in a chair. His blue eyes glittered as I came stumbling in propelled by Blair's hands, but when I spoke his name he turned his marred face away. He did not speak.

"Sit down, Carmichael," Martin said. "And don't move if you don't want to be hurt."

I obeyed automatically, conscious only of Ligny opposite me across the table.

"Say something, Lewis, for God's sake," I said.

Slumped forward, his bowed head jerking to the jostling of the yacht, he had the look of one denuded of resource or volition or even the power to care.

"He has nothing to say," Martin said.

"There is nothing he can say," Blair said.

I sourly contemplated them—Martin, blond, tousled, thick; Blair with his coppery hair and fighter's chin and fighting body. At this moment they were twins in their tough enjoyment of their triumph.

"So you've beaten him up," I said. "When is my turn coming?"

"Don't be so bloody stupid," Martin said. "There has been no beating up and there won't be. It's not in our books and, besides, there hasn't been time for that. We've only just got here, as you well know; you watched us from the headland."

It was no occasion for self-recrimination, but if I had read

161

the riddle of Ligny's lake, I would have been here long before Martin and Blair. And then what would I have done? What could I have done? Merely to tell Ligny that at last I knew he was a triple murderer?

"There's another thing too," Martin said. He paused. A flurry of wind funneled into the cavern and the yacht shuddered. "Miss Hancock would never agree to rough handling."

"Where *is* Miss Hancock?" I said.

"Don't be alarmed," Martin said. "Miss Hancock is safe in her cabin. After all, she doesn't want to see Captain Ligny, she says, not even to glance at him, which will be awkward for the next two or three days. But that's her decision. . . . Listen to me, Carmichael. Blair and I came here fully prepared to make Captain Ligny punish himself for what he did to Hugh Martin, Wilfrid Giles and Garrett Blair. In short, to kill himself. If he was a real man, he would have done away with himself long ago. . . ."

Ligny lifted his head and the bright saloon lamps shone on his scarred face. He deliberately looked at Martin, then at Blair and then at me. As far as I could tell, he betrayed no sign of emotion.

"Miss Hancock," resumed Martin, "has insisted on a compromise. We will take Captain Ligny back to the mainland and hand him over to the police authorities with all the evidence we have against him, including the evidence of his disappearance at Batemans Bay. I don't know what the police will do about a crime twenty-eight years old, but they'll have something to say about Batemans Bay."

There was a lurch of water under the yacht and then Blair leaned on the table and poked his face into mine.

"Fair enough, eh, Carmichael?" he rasped. "More than fair," he said, straightening up.

"And will I also be handed over to the police when we get back to the mainland?" I asked.

"You won't be coming back with us," Martin said. "You are staying here till your fisherman comes to fetch you next

Friday week. And by that time there will be nothing you can do about Captain Ligny."

A flame burned in Ligny's blue eyes and he spoke for the first time since, for all I knew, I saw him at Festival Hall. His voice was slow and rusty.

"Don't call me captain," he croaked. "Call me anything else but that."

"Captain, of course, is synonymous with murderer," Blair said.

A little spark sprang into life in my mind. It flared into a splendid beacon illuminating the peaks of memory, and the discrepancies of the letter resolved themselves. If *I* had been threatened with death, I would have done rather more than leave behind evidence of my murder.

The rays of the beacon reached down into the chasms of my troubled thinking. Though some dark perplexities remained, the shadow of the great unconformity between Captain Ligny and Lewis Ligny vanished.

A gust of wind came thundering into the cavern. When the noise had subsided, I stood up. "Bring Miss Hancock in here, Martin," I said.

"I will not—"

"For God's sake, don't argue. Just get her in at once. And get that gun out of sight before she sees it."

Martin hesitated, then putting the pistol away, he nodded at Blair, and Blair disappeared into the after companion. I did not look at Ligny and nobody spoke until Miss Hancock came in, Blair stepping in her wake. Bracing herself against the swaying of the yacht, she gave me a dark glance of surprise.

"Why, Mr. Carmichael!" she said.

And then she saw Ligny roped in the chair. I thought she was going to collapse, but as Wilfrid Giles had written, she was not the fainting kind.

"You could have warned me, Mr. Carmichael," she said.

"I've known it myself for only a few minutes, Miss Hancock."

163

"Known what?" Martin demanded.

"That this gentleman," I said, "is really Wilfrid Giles."

At that moment a tremendous buffet of wind and wave shook the yacht from stem to stern and all we could think of was saving our lives.

14

On my last trek to the southwest corner, alone on Coupe Island, when the wind was again tumbling waves into the cavern to collide with the backwash of their predecessors and go on to crash against the inner rampart and then bounce back, I was to marvel at our escape.

The phenomenon was all the more astonishing in that it was Ligny—no, Wilfrid Giles now—who rescued us. In the first seconds of desperate endeavor, I cut the ropes from him and staggered out onto the sleet-driven deck to hack away the moorings. There Blair joined me. When we fought our way back inside, Giles and Miss Hancock and Martin were in the wheelhouse, and Giles was at the wheel. There was no one to challenge his right. He was familiar from of old with the deadly traps and quirks of these waters and he knew what to do. The engines rumbling, he brought the yacht around, glissaded sideways on a crosscurrent, skirted a jagged reef, headed out to sea and swung south and east and north for the fiord.

We made the yacht fast in the dark haven off the main branch of the fiord; then we sat down in the saloon to drink hot coffee and eat sandwiches of meat and cheese. The gale roared a rough monody over the cliffs, and shrill descanting downdrafts jetted into the crevices, but in the saloon there was silence.

A silence in which the terror of the sea was forgotten in the shock of realizing that a man who had been pursued relentlessly did not exist. I'm all right, I thought; though there was still much I didn't understand, I had accomplished my mission. But the others?

I studied them covertly. Martin on my right around the table corner; over against me, Blair; Miss Hancock, sitting opposite to Martin; Giles (it was still hard to think of him as Giles) beside me on the same side of the table. All of them adjusting, breaking out from the habit of thought and emotion of twenty-eight years and making overgreat efforts to adapt to the new shape of things. The process brought stress and the stress burst out from Martin.

"Why?" he exploded at Giles.

"Why?" Giles repeated after a pause.

"You could have told me right at first in Canberra," Martin said. "I don't like being a fool. More"—he had difficulty with his voice—"I don't like to be in the position of having to apologize. I don't like to feel I'm a bastard."

I am not and never will be an aficionado of Edmund Martin, but by implication he had excluded Miss Hancock and Malcolm Blair from the malevolence he was admitting, and so I decided to forego the plug in the jaw I owed him.

"Why?" Giles said again in a lonely voice. "I killed Ligny —the real Ligny, and I've paid for it ever since."

The gale whooped over the fiord uninterrupted for half a minute; then Miss Hancock said, "We would like to hear your side of the story, Wilfrid."

His disfigured face turned to her as though in surprise at hearing the sound of his first name.

"It would be hard to make you understand without seeing the actual scene," he said. "And the weather is too rough to go and look."

166

"We could do the second best thing," Martin said. He went to the chart cabinet, brought out the relief map of Coupe Island and smoothed it out on the table. "There," he said, pointing at the "field of operations" between the sixth and seventh ridges.

Giles nodded as he contemplated the map, his face puckered with memory. He began to talk and before long we were back in the observers' bunker, waiting that still black November night with the seven men—the three observers and the four students—Captain Ligny, Hugh Martin, Wilfrid Giles and Garrett Blair. The scene came alive. The faces in the light of the torches. The distribution of typewritten sheets. The intense study for five minutes. The gathering up of the sheets. The issuing of colored torches and water pistols. The pressure of hate with Sergeant Giles surreptitiously fingering the small cashbox under his battle dress.

He made us see and hear. Sergeant Blair had been the first to depart from the bunker, and so Sergeant Giles, reasoning that Blair had the farthest to go, knew his destination was the southwest corner. W.O. Martin had been the second to leave the bunker. The northwest corner, Sergeant Giles had thought, because he himself had been allotted the southeast corner. Then it had been his turn to go and he knew without any shadow of doubt where Captain Ligny would be bound for—the northeast corner.

These facts established in his mind, Sergeant Giles had gone to his starting point and had hidden the cashbox holding the letter to Miss Hancock, but instead of waiting the few minutes to zero hour, he had set off to stalk Captain Ligny.

("Why?" asked Martin.

"Not to kill him," Giles said. "I only wanted to stop him killing me. And Blair and Martin too.")

At zero hour, he had followed Captain Ligny into the "field of operations," creeping through the trenches twenty feet behind his quarry. For a while he had thought that Captain Ligny had no inkling he was being trailed. Then Sergeant

Giles had made a disastrous mistake. He had discovered a trip wire attached to a machine gun ("a tommy gun"). According to the instructions, the students had to deactivate every weapon they encountered and he had assumed that Captain Ligny would have dealt with the tommy gun. But he hadn't and when Sergeant Giles went to move the wire out of the way, the tommy gun had opened up right above his head.

His mind had become a whirlwind of incoherent thinking. His folly in touching the wire. The realization that Captain Ligny had known all along he was being followed. Thought of the observers waiting for a telltale signal. Thoughts of other and deadlier traps ahead, of lethal blows on his neck (he had already experienced Captain Ligny's prowess in that regard), of murderous hands coming at him out of the dark.

He had panicked, flashed his torch (in the same instant knowing he was making another mistake in showing an orange signal in the wrong territory) and crawled off to his own area.

("That signal was duly noted," Martin said. "Two observers said it was orange. The other said it was red—Captain Ligny's."

"I heard what they said at the Court of Inquiry," said Giles. The floodgates were raised and he was speaking freely. "I had nothing to say, but that orange flash was responsible for what happened afterwards.")

His return to his rightful place had been uneventful, but he had tripped a rifle as soon as he got there. However, it had not mattered because at the same time two other students also ran into trouble—a flamethrower, he thought in looking back, and a land mine, and he had no qualms in signaling he was the cause of the rifle.

Recovered somewhat from his panic, he had remembered it was time for the students to reveal their progress to the observers. He had flashed his orange signal and though he missed any sign of the green and the blue, he had spotted a glow of red—around a corner in the trench he himself was in.

Thereupon he had resumed his stalking of Captain Ligny.

Rounding the corner on hands and knees, he had heard a delicate metallic tapping no more than fifteen feet away. He had listened for a few seconds; then a frightful glimmer of what was happening had dawned on him.

"Captain Ligny!" he had shouted. "I know what you're doing. Stop it! Stop it, damn you!"

He paused, looked down at the map and then glanced slowly around at his audience—Miss Hancock, Blair, Martin and me. I became conscious again of the howling gale and the creaking of the yacht's timbers. Giles's face was mottled—red on the few spots that had escaped the fire, glistening white on the scars.

"I was too late," he said. "Have you ever seen a flame-thrower in action? This was a portable one and I saw Captain Ligny in its glow, standing on a fire step below it. He had manipulated it so that the recoil sent it spinning and spurting fire for a hundred feet around. There was a dugout beside him so he could jump into it when the thrower enfiladed the trench we were in. I heard screams through the noise and I knew poor Blair and Martin had gone. And so was Captain Ligny. I jumped at him from the back, dragged him from the firestep and when the thrower had swiveled round, I threw him into the path of the fire. And then he screamed himself."

He stopped abruptly. The gale swooped and shrieked over the cliffs. Malcolm Blair stood up, went to the saloon's bar and returned to place a glass of whiskey in front of Giles. Glancing around inquiringly, he received no demurs and so we all sat sipping whiskey.

"The orange flash," Miss Hancock said at last.

Giles turned to look her squarely in the face.

" 'I would not stand between any man and his genius,' " he said. "Do you remember who wrote that?"

Miss Hancock was startled and a little scared.

"I can't exactly recall," she said hesitantly, but I saw she did know the answer.

169

Giles turned to me.

"What about you? Do you remember?"

"It was written by Henry David Thoreau," I said.

"He wasn't talking about me and *my* genius," Giles said. "My genius let me down and more than once. I should have followed Captain Ligny into the fire. I should have, but I was afraid and I dived into the dugout and I cried. I cried with the pain of my burnt face, for I'd got my share of the Greek fire, and when I touched my chin burned skin came away."

He took several deep breaths.

"But in the pain," he went on doggedly, "*despite* the pain, I thought of my orange flash. I thought of the observers. They would be racing down from the bunker and when they saw what had happened to the thrower, they would remember the orange signal in Captain Ligny's area and there was only one thing they could think. *I* was responsible for the sabotage. *I* was responsible for the killing of three men. . . . My genius was a coward. When the thrower went quiet, I went out into the trench and changed identities with Captain Ligny."

It had been comparatively easy to effect. Captain Ligny was a charred hulk. His captain's cloth pips had been incinerated with his shirt and it was simple for Sergeant Giles to take off his own shirt and hurl it into the fire still raging. He had also thrown the water pistols into the fire. Strangely Captain Ligny's "disc identity" and his wristwatch had come through in recognizable form and there had been no difficulty in swapping them with Sergeant Giles's disc and watch. As for his face, well, the flamethrower had taken care of that.

And when, later, he had understood that he had been in no danger of being denounced as a murderer, it was too late to do anything but live the rest of his life as Captain Ligny, and he had let the plastic surgeons do what they liked about his face.

Then he jumped forward twenty-eight years. With many hesitations he said he had been still under the thrall of living

170

as Captain Ligny when he blew up the dugouts last night. The cashbox and the letter had not yet been found and he had to make sure they couldn't be found. He had to destroy any evidence leading to the uncovering of his real identity.

And if we couldn't understand that, he said with the old desperate appeal in his eyes, we did not have any conception of guilt. By guilt, though he did not say this explicitly, he wasn't thinking of his killing Captain Ligny but of his failure to face up to the consequences when the killing had occurred.

"You've heard the story," he said, looking around at each of us in turn. "You might as well hear the start of it—the real start. You know what I mean?"

I didn't know, and Miss Hancock and Martin were no better off, but Malcolm Blair leaned forward urgently.

"I can guess," he said. "I haven't forgotten my father's letters. How—where you met Captain Ligny first. Am I right?"

Giles nodded, and once again we listened to a somber recital. Early in 1940 (I'm giving only the bare bones of this account), Sergeant Giles was attached to a training battalion on the Adelaide River near Darwin, and Captain Ligny, then a sergeant like Giles, had come to the battalion in a temporary capacity. There was a crowd of aborigines in the Adelaide River bush, declared out of bounds to troops: no fraternization was permitted. One night a crocodile got a young lubra, and a party of soldiers, including Sergeant Giles, took her out of the river next morning—what was left of her. But that night Sergeant Giles had seen Ligny with the lubra beforehand and he knew, though he couldn't prove it, that Ligny had clubbed the girl and thrown her into the river. This he had told to Ligny, and why, as well, and so there had begun the great hate between them. But before any serious fracas could develop, Ligny was returned to his own unit down south and Sergeant Giles had written off his hate as a bad memory, only to have it revived horribly when he reported in at Royal Park and found Ligny, now a captain, in life and

171

death control over him, and Garrett Blair and Hugh Martin too.

"So there it is," said Giles.

It came to me, in the ensuing pause, that I could no longer hear the noise of the gale, that instead there was the low reverberation of waves rolling onto the foot of the cliffs. The same reduction of turbulence was needed in Giles and so I introduced matters of lesser importance.

"How did you trick me yesterday afternoon?" I asked.

He stared at me and then his lips twitched which was a good sign. He had been there all the time, he said, lying low in the bracken and waiting for me to go.

"And what about your supplies? Where are they?"

"At the southwest base," he replied. Then, with a quick glance at Martin, he said, "As Mr. Martin has seen, there is room in the cavern to camp a score of men."

"But it must have been quite a job unloading your stuff here and then lumping it to the other end of the island."

Nothing so strenuous as that, he said. He had unloaded the supplies directly from his yawl in the cavern and afterwards he had brought the yawl around here.

"The cavern," he went on, "is no place to keep a boat—as you now know."

The tension had appreciably slackened, but Martin very nearly sent it soaring up again.

"Mr. Giles," he said, "we are now in the position of having to crawl on our knees abjectly. And we've got to think of getting you—and us—out of this fix, but there is a question or two to answer. For instance, why did you go to Festival Hall?"

The bone-hard strain was back in Giles's face.

"I suppose that had to come," he said. "I wanted to look at Garrett Blair's son for the last time. You"—he looked at Malcolm Blair—"are very like your father, you know."

"But why?" persisted Martin.

In a tired voice, Giles again launched into self-revelation, the genius that had betrayed him when he took on the guise of Captain Ligny, that also had betrayed him when he ran away from Batemans Bay instead of ending it all in the sea. But the genius was not altogether bad. From afar, as it were, he had watched over Garrett Blair's son and taken care of him. He had secretly helped him from time to time, sending money to him through Legacy (at this, Malcolm Blair's face was scarlet) and as the boy grew and developed into a champion fighter and a decent man, he had found some consolation and amnesty from remorse.

As he spoke, I could see that Malcolm Blair was recalling the bitter speeches he had made to me about Ligny. He would have spoken of this, but I caught his eye in time and shook my head.

"Thank you," Martin said to Giles. "There is another matter. Perhaps to Carmichael here, it's no mystery, but why did you build your model lake in the shape of Walden Pond?"

I had called it an icon. There I had not been exactly right, as I discovered when Giles rather haltingly replied to Martin's question. More precisely, it was the sublimation of his wish to re-create a world in which the happiness of Walden Pond was transposed with the anguish of Coupe Island as he had transposed the land of Coupe Island with the water of his little lake. A make-believe world in which Captain Ligny had never existed. He did not enlarge on the theme and there was no need.

One question remained. It belonged to Miss Hancock, but as she apparently did not intend to enter her claim, I asked it myself.

"Lewis—I mean, Wilfrid, how did Miss Hancock's *Walden* get into your possession?"

"I stole it," he said, "when I saw the shape of Walden Pond coincided with the shape of the model Captain Ligny made us work on. Besides—I'm also fond of Thoreau. I'm sorry, Miss Hancock."

Miss Hancock stayed unresponsive.

Blair left his chair and circled the table with decanter and carafe and refilled the glasses. He sat down and said, "Well, what's to be done now?"

There was no reply and his big hand heavily tapped the table.

"For God's sake," he demanded, "isn't there anybody with ideas? We just can't leave Mr. Giles here for the rest of his life. What about you yourself, Mr. Giles?"

Giles merely shook his head.

"There's only one thing for it," I said. "Mr. Ligny was drowned at Batemans Bay. Mr. Ligny has to come to life again and you're the man to arrange it, Martin."

"Explain," said Martin coldly.

"Amnesia. You find or arrange somebody to find Mr. Ligny in some remote place on the mainland suffering a loss of memory covering the last two weeks or so. He can't say where he has been or how or why. And the people—ten of them, isn't it—who know what actually happened will not talk."

"Very good, Mr. Carmichael," applauded Miss Hancock. "Very, very good. Mr. Martin, you will see to it, won't you?"

Martin's clever, calculating eyes sought Giles.

"What's your opinion, Mr. Giles?"

"I'm in your hands. I can't do anything myself."

"What I mean is, Could you play the amnesia game successfully?"

"I've been acting for twenty-eight years," Giles said wearily.

"Very well." Martin spent a few moments in thought. "There are hurdles," he said. "Where to have you found; the medical examination; the legal unscrambling; reinstatement in your job—if you want it. But the real problem is the yawl. Where's the yawl's home port?"

Giles drew the correct inference.

"I own it," he said. "I didn't hire it or steal it. As for the home port, I kept it at Williamstown near Melbourne."

"Where, of course, it is registered in the name of Lewis Ligny?"

174

"No," Giles said. "I always felt it was inevitable I had to come back to Coupe Island. Years ago I registered the yawl under another name."

"Your face," said Martin, "is distinctive. We can't have people at Williamstown identifying the man found suffering from amnesia. It's a million to one against anybody from Williamstown, or anywhere else, coming here, but we can't take the chance. Do you agree?"

So, though it went sorely against the grain, we went out onto the landing and reduced the yawl to anonymous wreckage.

During the night, the storm fled to the east and morning discovered Coupe Island to be the center of a blue, lazily undulating sea. Supervised by inquisitive gulls, I stood on the cliff above the little shingly beach where Amos Waller had landed me and I watched the *Erica* heading north with much blaring of the klaxon.

Miss Hancock, Wilfrid Giles and Malcolm were on the deck, but I couldn't see Martin, out of sight in the wheelhouse. I would have liked to go with them, but I had, of course, to stay on the island until Amos Waller came to fetch me, inquiring no doubt about wildlife on Coupe Island.

When the yacht had shrunk to a distant white speck, I turned to go back to the hut. A long warm sleep first, I thought, to make up for lost hours, and afterwards days of leisurely exploration of Coupe Island. Then I thought of the farewells exchanged before the *Erica* had backed out of the fiord.

First, Martin's:

"We're not popular with each other," he said, his smiling superior-self regained. "Let me know when you're coming to Canberra and I'll get out of the way."

He was right open for a king hit, but I regretfully waived the opportunity.

Then Blair's:

175

"I'm looking for you at Mahon's Crossing in the near future, Sandy. But wait a couple of weeks. At the moment the place is overrun with Legacy kids."

Then Wilfrid Giles's:

"I'm sorry about Festival Hall," he said. "I could only think of one thing there. Do you understand?"

"Of course."

"How can I make up for everything?"

"What about giving me a complete rundown in managing Ligny's lake?"

"Whenever you are ready," he said, and we shook hands.

Finally Miss Hancock's:

On the landing, she drew me out of earshot of the others. Her furry hat was perched on her white head, her black eyes sparkled and her pink-gold skin glowed rosily.

"Thank you," she said. "I was afraid you would betray our secret yesterday, but I shouldn't have worried."

"Betray?" I said.

"Please forgive me," she said. "I take the word back. When the Hancocks bury the past, they want it to stay buried, and there is something of the Hancocks in you, Mr. Carmichael."

Belatedly perceiving the important word was not *betray,* but *secret,* I had a premonition of all gaps ready to be filled in. The curious gaps in Miss Hancock's diary. Quentin Hancock's strange introduction of the four soldiers to Worriong Cottage. Elspeth's quick espousal of the cause of the three N.C.O.'s against their officer. Her weeping over the battered Wilfrid Giles in Mick's Hollow. Miss Hancock's sturdy denial of a love affair between Elspeth and Giles. These fell into place and more, as well.

"So?" I said.

"So we'll never talk about this again," Miss Hancock said. "But after all these years, I'm happy to get my nephew back and I really don't care if he's called Wesley Hancock, Wilfrid Giles or Lewis Ligny. As it is, it's got to be Ligny, but I won't complain."

176